MW00974254

The Men at Golgotha-
The Two Christ Loved

JOSEPH LEWIS

Text Copyright © 2014 Joseph Lewis

Cover Art "A Thief's Table" Copyright © 2016 Joseph Lewis

All rights reserved.

No part of this book may be reproduced in any form or by any means without the prior written consent of the Publisher, excepting brief quotes used in reviews. Poetic license has been used in forming the characters that are known to be in the original text of the Bible. While many of the names are fictional, the integrity of God's word is kept. Any similarities of these fictional names and/or events are completely coincidental.

Published by Lewis & Verb LLC
www.josephlewisbooks.com

ISBN: 0692659900
ISBN-13: 978-0692659908

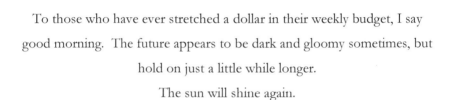

To those who have ever stretched a dollar in their weekly budget, I say good morning. The future appears to be dark and gloomy sometimes, but hold on just a little while longer.

The sun will shine again.

CONTENTS

Acknowledgments   i

Preface   1

1   Chapter One   4

2   Chapter Two   15

3   Chapter Three   23

4   Chapter Four   36

5   Chapter Five   42

6   Chapter Six   49

7   Chapter Seven   61

8   Chapter Eight   68

9   Chapter Nine   83

10   Chapter Ten   91

11   Chapter Eleven   96

12   Chapter Twelve   103

13   Chapter Thirteen   114

14   Chapter Fourteen   117

15   Chapter Fifteen   121

16   Chapter Sixteen   133

17   Chapter Seventeen   137

Afterword   149

ACKNOWLEDGMENTS

To my God - thank you. I would like to make a special shout out to Miss Margaret Johnson-Hodge for being willing to share your wisdom and designing the front cover. To Mrs. Avis Marshall and Ms. Jahana Martin, thank you for your precision and expertise. To Michael Lancette for being a true artist and creating a masterpiece for the cover, thank you. To Kaitlynn Lewis, thank you for your support and designing the back cover. And to the chosen few that knew I was writing this book before I wrote my first page - thanks.

PREFACE

There are many stories about Jesus and His impact on humanity. We can also learn from His disciples and their teachings, trials and tribulations. However, there is little to be said about the two men who died just a few feet from Jesus. I've always wondered why this was so. These men were not heaven-sent individuals. They came from a natural birth. They started this life just like the rest of us, yet mysteriously, they are joined with Christ at His execution. So was it random, pre-ordained, or simply a mere coincidence that they died so close to Jesus?

During my research I found the following verses about the robbers: Matthew 27:38-44; Mark 15:27-28; Luke 23:32-43; John 19:18, 31-33. After reading the Gospels, I remained puzzled about the two robbers who died with the Messiah. Yet somehow the scriptures inspired me to write about these two men. Take a few minutes and read those passages in your spare time and you'll see what I mean. According to scripture, we are briefly acquainted with the last few moments of their lives, and interestingly enough, we only know small parts of that.

I truly believe that these thieves, like many other people who are in the Bible, were mentioned so that the readers of the book can use their imagination. Why? So we can apply their events to our own lives and keep ourselves accountable. God can use anyone for His glory, and He truly gets all of it.

In telling their hypothetical story, I am not attempting to glorify larceny or encouraging the masses to do so. Those men paid the ultimate price for their actions, but why did they do it? Surely, being adults, they knew the difference between right and wrong. Yet when we look back on our lives, why do we do the things we do especially when we know it is wrong in the first place?

So as the story begins, there was a text written by an angel that chronicled the details of this tale from the robbers' point-of-view. The angel never identifies himself, but he was in the presence of both men during the preceding days of their fate. He describes how they were sentenced to death, the night before the crucifixion, and Good Friday from their perspective. God has formed this angel with a grand core, strong enough to carry men and women of any size, and with wings greater than those of an eagle. When duty calls, a long and sharp sword sits by his waist for easy access. This angel typically carries himself with a militant demeanor, using his strength and his presence to fulfill his only purpose. However, God decides to alter his routine. Instead of limiting his service to spiritual gifts, God instructs the narrator to make reports of everything he witnesses. He is equipped with a holy scroll, so that he can compose accurate notes.

I wondered, from whom did the crooks decide to steal from and why did they do it? Were they unaware of the consequences that result from such actions? Were they simply hooligans? Then I began to think: are these burglars so similar to 'regular people' that we feel uncomfortable acknowledging they exist within our own circles of society? Do we make the same mistakes they've made? And, is it possible to learn about Christ through them? In order to address all of this, I would like to present one version of the men's story. Due to the context of when this account was written, the narrator uses one of the debated transliterations of the Aramaic/Hebrew name of Jesus. In short, when the name "Yahshua" appears, think "Jesus."

After so many years, the untold story is coming to light. Praise God. There was so much attention to detail, that I didn't know where to start. Instead of changing the story to my liking, the author and I decided to give the text in its unedited form. During their life, they both had a big decision to make.

CHAPTER ONE

After he had found the treasury and broken the lock, he hastily grabbed as many coins as he could. His soul was filled with a silent joy as his fists overflowed with gold, silver, and copper coins. He placed all of them into a plain sack which he had hidden within his robe. Fearful of getting caught, he decided not to take anymore. The cunning and crafty man managed to climb out of a window with all of his money and barely make a sound. The thief acted with caution because he knew the next steps would be the most critical in his plan. His only goal was a simple and sweet victory. If he could escape the danger of being seen, he would be able to savor his newly found riches. The thief leaned against the wall and glanced around a corner, curious as to who may have been on the other side. He observed where the moonlight hit the ground to guide his next footsteps. This man had to avoid the lit areas at all costs.

He whispered to himself, "You have come this far, Jonarbi. Your family needs you home safe. They also need this money."

The man remained quiet and hid himself in the darkness. He watched his surroundings carefully. Even though his escape was now within his grasp, his refuge resided across the pathway on the other side of a small field. Jonarbi had no idea that I had watched him execute his entire plan.

As I composed Jonarbi's story in my holy scroll, I felt another presence lurking amongst us. Although Jonarbi was ignorant of its existence, he would soon be haunted by it. I put my writings away and reached to my side. I calmly drew my sword and took a strong, defensive stance. There was a legion of dark shadows headed in our direction, crawling lightly on the blades of grass.

As the demons encircled the corrupt man, one of them told me, "Tonight will mark his doom. You are looking at a dead man."

I responded, "Jonarbi is still alive. He is in my Father's hands."

The demon said, "Your Father confirmed this? I don't see His presence here. I only see one man with another man's money. I am sure He wouldn't allow this terrible thing to happen. God is not here. There is no god here, or anywhere for that matter."

"My Father is the God of the living. Jonarbi is still alive because of His grace."

"This is madness! Surely he is good as dead as of tonight. If he is caught, he will die. And, if Jonarbi is not arrested tonight, he will be cursed."

I had enough of hearing anything that this demon had to say. As I lifted the blade of my sword, I counted the spirits around me. There were five of them. Not wanting to test my patience, two of them walked off to be near the thief. They crouched next to Jonarbi and started to put thoughts into his head. The other three remained near me.

The demon to the left said, "This man is wise. A fool acts in compulsion, but Jonarbi has put much thought into stealing this money. We adore his precepts. It makes everything that much more enjoyable for us."

"Silence. I am fully aware of the man's plans, but I am more concerned with God's plan," I responded.

The demon asked, "Does it hurt you to watch his destruction come to pass? I know who you are and why you are here, and I watched your holiness meddle in our affairs."

"Unfortunately, Jonarbi has dwelled on these evil thoughts for too long. I was there when the seed was planted. It was here at this temple. You were here also. He went inside with the right intentions, to receive counsel for his issues, a helping hand, the truth and the light in his dark hour," I answered. "Yet you tainted what he saw. Jonarbi saw men and women reach into their cloaks and bring out coins. He witnessed the money being dropped into the basket. The sound of the coins played a song for Jonarbi. He had watched two men take the money to another room to count all of the newly collected riches. This memory played in his mind and his heart many times. Jonarbi felt that the hairs on his head were outnumbered by his desperate need for money."

"No one can escape their trust in money. No one has escaped our trap, and no one ever will. We will kill him and you will witness it soon enough. There will be death, or why would you be here?"

"I am here to carry out His orders not mine."

The moon shined brightly and the stars lit up the sky. I raised my eyes towards the heavens, past the moon and stars to receive my instructions. Should I fight, do I take a life or do I stand still? I waited patiently for His response while I kept the yielded sword on guard. Once I received my instructions I lowered the blade. My attention returned to watching the man. Jonarbi lifted his eyes over the bush to see if it was still safe to stand. He then stood and pressed himself on the wall. He quickly proceeded towards the corner of the building.

Jonarbi's goal was just a few moments away. He closed his eyes and muttered the names of his family in a whisper. After the fifth name, he cast his lot and took a quick glance around the corner of the building. Seizing the moment, Jonarbi used all his might and all of his strength to run across the field. One of his arms swung with haste while the other remained somewhat still. In an effort to make a successful run, he kept his other hand clinched on his treasures. He made sure none of his coins fell out during his escape. The money barely made a sound.

As he fled from the scene of the crime, Jonarbi ran a distinct path across the field. Once he reached an area filled with trees, he made turns to the left and then to the right. Although he appeared to run aimlessly, he was looking for large rocks on the ground. For these points told him whether he should run right or left, depending on which side of the tree the rock was placed. His efforts led him through the darkness. I followed the man closely and the demons were led with increasing interests of his heart.

When the man arrived at the end of the wooded area, he slowed down to gather himself, yet remained vigilant. After observing the open road, he walked with determination towards a cluster of homes. His eyes narrowed upon one. Jonarbi disregarded the time of the night and knocked on the door continuously. Once a voice answered the knock, Jonarbi paused and took inventory of the other properties.

A man opened the door asking, "Why do you come so late? I will not be faithful in my work tomorrow morning."

"Pardon my late arrival. My children kept me busy at home today. Surely you understand how that can be, Brutus."

"I beg of you, don't remind me."

Brutus opened the door wide enough for only Jonarbi, but the demons simply walked through the walls of the humble home. I followed Jonarbi closely while they headed to a room filled with food. The host had started to eat without Jonarbi. When Jonarbi sat at his table, Brutus reached for the new wine skins. He filled some cups full of the dark red wine.

"I see that you truly have been blessed. You haven't missed any meals," the host stated.

"Have I become a glutton? My eating habits haven't changed in years," Jonarbi added.

"Well, I see that bulge within your robe. It is either too much rich food prepared at your table, or you are trying to conceal something."

"I have no secrets, old friend." As Jonarbi reached into his robe to unveil his riches, he added, "I had to meet a few new customers today. Unfortunately, I had no time to make a deposit."

"Today was a prosperous day. I am not the smartest businessman in the world, but that appears to be three months' wages, perhaps even four."

"I suppose I had great opportunities and favor today. The gods met in secret and concluded to assist my livelihood. For what reason, I do not know," Jonarbi said.

"We know their plans as much as we know the results of casting our lots. Yet again, how would we ever know that someone or something controls our madness? Yesterday, I attained quick earnings. I won one hundred silver quinarii, a great way to start the week."

"Money will always be the source of how we function. Here's to our wealth and our deaths, for both are certain and both are glorious."

The men raised their cups and nodded in agreement. As I wrote in the holy scroll, the demons were delighted by the conversation. They walked around the men in curiosity, while they continued to plant small thoughts into Jonarbi's head. Although the men had only one drink, the dark shadows were shifting his attention from the fermented drink to the enjoyment of having company.

As the head of the household replenished their cups, he said, "I am glad to see that your efforts have turned your situation around. A good man must always provide for his family, and you have not failed them. Those that do not provide should be thrown into Hades."

"I could not say it better. We must do what it takes no matter what."

"Since your business is obviously doing better, have you begun to seek a new business partner? Such an arrangement could bring forth more riches with new perspective and you could move…"

"No. I cannot and will not have one."

"Why is this so?"

"I cannot trust anyone anymore. You are the closest to that person, and I still deny these thoughts."

"Jonarbi, you may be the smartest person in any given room when it comes to handling business. But because of your stiff-necked ways, I believe that this is also your greatest weakness."

"How dare you say such things? Explain yourself, Brutus."

"Do not let *pride* get in your way. Let the past go. Everyone needs counsel, but only the wise seek it out. Everyone else can only marvel at their own foolishness."

"History can only repeat itself when its records are not taken into account. In one hand, I see my success and how I produced my income. It was my plans and discernment in business that brought me things. On the other hand, I see where I have fallen on ground that was not fertile, and I see where my toil has been for naught. How could I move forward without these truths? A new partner will only slow me down. I will come out of this sluggish patch. I see myself riding on fine horses and chariots with honor and glory."

"I agree that you have a few months' wages in your possession, yet it won't get you rich overnight. Be steady plodding and pace yourself. Why have the finest chariot and lose your home?" Brutus asked

Jonarbi answered, "Unfortunately, I need more sums of money like this. The weight of the money lenders is unbearable. I also have doubts about the profits increasing with another hand making a withdrawal for his share."

"I hear your concerns. If such weight were upon my shoulders, I would do anything it takes to pay my debt. I'd fear that my wife and daughters could become another man's servant, or worse, a slave. I have kept minimal contact in my life with money lenders, yet it is a fear that will never go away. Those lazy sluggards live life lavishly at another's expense. I loathe them."

"In my heart I envy them. Could you imagine what life would be like if we were on the receiving end of the deal? The possibilities could be endless."

Brutus raised his glass. "This cup is for the hated money lender."

After finishing their last sip, Brutus offered Jonarbi another drink. Their conversation slowed. The wine was great in color yet the size of the cups could not satisfy their thirst. The skins were lifted to pour each of them another ration, then a fourth, fifth, and a sixth. I watched their laughs increase in extended periods and their smiles widen with red-stained teeth.

"These fools are truly one of us," one demon said to another. "They are controlled by only what feels good, and what seems right. Surely, Jonarbi and Brutus will drink to unawareness."

Another dark shadow stated, "This is great for us. Even though Jonarbi has escaped the eyes of others, he will definitely stumble. His plan will come to the dreaded light. He will bring ruin upon himself."

The hour had come when Jonarbi felt enough time had passed since his deed. Jonarbi requested one more drink before he left. While insisting that he have one last drink to put his mind at ease, the host brought bowls to the table and began pouring. Both men chuckled. One of them stated that he had not enjoyed this many drinks in a long time. The other said it was when he was a much younger man that he had done so. Without any words to remember the days of old, the bowls were lifted and immediately indulged.

"Is 'Sweet Victory' the name of this flavor?" asked Jonarbi.

"It should be. You should know, for it is your wine. I mean it is yours that's mine, no, no, it is my wine of which that I've paid for that, you understand what I mean," Brutus slurred.

"Of course, yes, I recognize my own finished product. I just…I just…I-I sometimes wait an extended period of time before I drink the choice wine, especially drink heavily. Tell me my friend: is it destiny that we end up like this from time to time?"

"If, if you are referred…referring to drinking past our regular tolerance, then no. We are…are both hard men with hard lives and high tolerances to match."

"Allow me to clarify. What think came—I mean what happened first: our appetite and desire to drink for a thirst that cannot be quenched or is…is it the *problems* we face that cause us to drink past our limits of satisfaction?"

"I don't know Jonarbi. We are not old men, but our lives are rugged. We walk this life within crooked lines in the absence of light to guide us. We've done the best we can. I know I'm still alive because if I…since you had…I raise my cup of wine in spite of life's bitter taste. And you are going to do the same and continue to live on, for years to come. Your efforts for family and yourself won't be in vain. Don't be too hard on yourself."

I continued to write more notes in my holy scroll. The demons remained an invisible terror to Jonarbi. The two men talked as though they hadn't seen each other in a long time, but their will to speak had become challenged.

Jonarbi asked, "How is Joshua doing? I haven't seen…haven't…have not seen him for a long…"

"Joshua? Yes, yes he is going to be a father soon," Brutus answered.

"That is good. You know—you—I…I haven't seen him since the

wedding."

"Now that was a celebration worth every-everything spent, Jonarbi. The couple looked so joyful. It's been years, brother...years since...since I had seen...since I've seen a married couple glow like that. The food and wine was rich and delicious. Thanks for giving Joshua a favorable price for the aged wine."

"Old wine was necessary for the occasion. My gift was for everyone to enjoy," Jonarbi said while he stood up. "When will your younger brother find his bride?"

"My brother has been engaged for some time to some whore woman. Soon there should be a..." Brutus said before being interrupted by a loud sound.

When Jonarbi made his way towards the front door, his hand carelessly let the money slip through his fingers. The sack of coins did not have a secure tie around the opening, allowing the money to spill all over the floor. The man fell to his knees, reaching aimlessly around the area to gather the riches. Brutus' eyes were dazzled by what he saw.

"These cursed coins," Jonarbi stated.

After regaining his composure, Brutus said, "I have never seen so many of them in one place. Here let me help you with this."

"No! I will clean this up; you're only going to stand in my way."

"Stand in your way is what you say, while you're in my house?! Have you gone mad?"

When Brutus handed over the collected money, Jonarbi reluctantly said, "Thank you, it's just that it went everywhere and I can't afford to lose any of it."

"Don't bother to explain because I know. Are you certain that all of this came from new customers?"

"Yes, indeed. Your brother isn't the only one to marry. Some of the interested parties had large gatherings to accommodate, which only created larger sums for me."

"Sounds like you may need some help with an event in the future."

"I will send a letter with the plans. I bid you good evening."

Jonarbi stepped outside and was refreshed by the cold and crisp air that hit his face. He checked to his left and to his right to see if anyone was around. He saw no reason to be concerned, and began his journey home. I followed Jonarbi's footsteps in the moonlit path. Further down the road he came across some other travelers of the night. He made sure to appear normal, and continued his stride down the road. However, the men who wore robes of Pharisees muttered something amongst themselves. Assuming the remark was about him; Jonarbi spat towards the sandals of the men and looked directly into their eyes. One man was disgusted with his act, but the other men encouraged him to ignore the offensive gesture and carry on. They wrote Jonarbi off as a local drunk, and did not waste their time.

As I wrote what I had witnessed, Jonarbi crossed paths with several Roman officials. I put the scroll within my robe and looked towards the heavens. Should I prepare for Jonarbi's downfall or should I watch with content? God responded with the latter, so I stood and watched. The officials had stern looks with cold eyes. When they inquired about where Jonarbi was headed, he answered with the name of his town. Jonarbi was anxious and clinched the money tighter. To his astonishment, the officials allowed him to go on his way. With newfound confidence in his executed robbery, he went home.

Jonarbi walked through his front door exhausted and breathed a sigh of relief. He went into his room where his wife was sound asleep and lay down beside her. She smiled slightly and murmured his name. After he acknowledged her, she returned to her slumber. I watched his fingers play with a silver denarii. He enjoyed the feeling of the weight in his hand. Time passed as he fell asleep from his drunken stupor, and the coin fell from his hand and rolled away. I asked my heavenly Father for guidance and he instructed me to take a life, but not Jonarbi's.

I made haste and went to a home a few arrow shots away. As I entered their room I saw an elderly couple in a deep sleep. My father desired to see the man, for he had believed and loved the Lord for a long time but now he was old. As he lay on his side, his arm embraced his wife. Unaware of what I was going to do, the man remained a protector keeping her safe and warm. His good works were now complete and I wanted to leave the memory of him as it stood. So as he took a final breathe, I pressed my hand on his shoulder. His chest fell and never rose again.

After God called the name of His servant, his spirit sat upright on his bed. I reassured him that he shouldn't be afraid, yet he had never seen anyone's glory shine so brightly so his look of awe remained. After I gave him my name, I extended my hand for him to take hold. The man already knew where we were heading. Once he arrived at the gates they opened and then closed promptly so unwanted guests wouldn't gain entrance. I pointed in the direction he should go to for judgment, and I told the man he had nothing to fear. His troubles were over.

Now that this job was finished, my orders were to continue to follow Jonarbi. My wings stretched wide as I began to travel back to earth when the man asked me if I was returning for his wife. I told him that her name has not been called by God; therefore she would remain alive, for now.

CHAPTER TWO

Each time I left Heaven, I knew I would return soon. Starting with the night Jonarbi committed larceny, my routine had not been the same. Ever since he walked home with riches, my orders had been to keep a close eye on him. Days had passed and God had given me various assignments to carry out. For each assignment, I made the journey to earth and then to heaven, but for Jonarbi I only watched.

His daily routine changed as well. During the first few days following the robbery, he grew exceedingly anxious of what was heard about the crime. Whenever the topic came up, Jonarbi appeared to be genuinely concerned about the unfortunate event, yet secretly he worried if there was suspicion towards him or a trail which led back his way. He casually received accounts from family, friends, and customers.

Life at home had been altered, slightly. To keep up an appearance of having steady income, Jonarbi resumed giving the same amounts of money to his wife for household needs. He also wasn't so harsh towards his wife and kids. Jonarbi had chosen to be content with the unearned gain, and withheld his right to complain about his debts. The burdens seemed to become lighter that way.

Jonarbi made extra efforts to conceal his evil deed from the money lenders. He blended the new gold, silver, and copper coins with the honest earnings, and made his regular scheduled payments to mimic that of a successful business. One day he walked into town to meet with a money lender to make a payment. Jonarbi was tall with broad shoulders. He walked with pride and dignity. His beard wasn't as long as the elders, yet his smile commanded the attention of the townsmen, women and children. The little boys and girls greeted him with great cheer as he walked by. When Jonarbi arrived, Satan appeared.

"Here's another payment," said Jonarbi.

"Thank you Jonarbi. I am sorry that my master couldn't make it. He was feeling ill this morning so I am standing in the gap today," the servant added. "You are making great progress with your debt. Business must be going well for you."

Jonarbi replied, "I had some new customers since we last met."

"Of course. The reputation of your aged wines has spread across the land. I might even make another purchase."

"Jonarbi will burn in Hades, you'll see," Satan told me. "I can see it now. I could smell the stench of his soul. My legion will feast upon him, forever."

"Only a fool would wish misery on another," I countered.

Satan exclaimed, "This man will not change! He would do whatever to keep his place in society. He lives for the respect from others, yet disrespects the same people. He is surely as wretched as one of us."

"Leave this place!"

As the devil laid his hand on the servant, he told me, "I will kill Jonarbi. Why do you question me? Do you trust in your lord? Trust me. He will die."

The devil vanished from my eyes and I returned my focus towards the two men. I had written the quick words that were being exchanged between the two.

"I am glad things are going so well for you now. We may join together to do more investments in the future. These days, it doesn't look like everyone is in the best of circumstances. Haven't you heard of what happened on the other side of town?" the servant asked.

"I was over there today before I came here and heard nothing. Was it something unfortunate?" Jonarbi replied.

"I am afraid so. The land over there is cursed. There was a robbery that stirred up fear in the people, and the strangest things occurred. Another robbery happened shortly after, and one the following day, and three more after that. No one has been captured or charged with the crimes."

"Those scoundrels," Jonarbi said knowing he was responsible for only one robbery.

"To make matters worse, no one knows if it was done by one thief or a few. Oh how I envy them. If I had enough motivation to…"

Jonarbi interjected, "Pardon me? What did you say? Why would you expose yourself to such danger?"

"This is for your ears only. If I could get away with any crime, it would be robbery. There's something unique about stealing."

"What is so unique about it?"

"Unlike the other crimes, there is an immediate and lasting payoff to the thief's bottom line. Think about it. That bandit got away without being caught. It only takes two people to witness a crime to be held and the suspect will be charged with a crime and punished. That thief obviously got away with the crime since nobody saw him. Therefore, he keeps all the spoils."

Jonarbi added, "I like your logic."

The servant laughed, "A man like me could use a few extra coins. Could you imagine me being a part of any of those thefts? You wouldn't even know it if I was standing in front of your face."

"I certainly wouldn't."

After Jonarbi's meeting, I looked towards heaven and received new orders. I departed for a little one who needed to meet with God up above. A baby girl had been overcome with sickness. Her struggle ended once my finger touched the sweat of her forehead. When God called her by name, my hands reached down for her spirit. She was too young to stand, so I cradled her in my arms. I took extra care when ascending to the heavens, while the parents cried out in dismay. I pray that they know their little one is with the Lord, where she is comforted in the sight of the wings of my brothers. The baby now crawls on the streets of gold smiling, where her Lord dwells forever.

The Lord released me from my normal duties to observe Jonarbi once again. I entered his home with my holy scroll in hand. The family was enjoying a bountiful feast. The children laughed loudly. Jonarbi's wife was content and smiled brightly. The man of the household, on the contrary, remained deep in thought as he picked at his meal. He began to wonder about what he would do when the money ran out.

His attention on the food was broken when he looked across the table. Jonarbi's wife looked so happy, despite everything that was happening financially. She couldn't care less about the money. Her eyes were filled with bliss. Jonarbi wished to have her mindset. This doubtful man begged to have peace for just one day.

In desperate search of the truth, Jonarbi lifted his voice asking, "How was your day with the children?"

She replied, "The children were fine. Why do you look this way? You didn't enjoy your food?"

"Of course I did. Everything is perfect. I have one question to ask you. Before I propose the question, let me tell you what I saw when I walked home. There were a few beggars that asked me for some copper coins.

Everything in me wanted to give, yet I withheld because of our current circumstances. Is this just? Am I cursed?" Jonarbi asked.

"No. We must do for ourselves. Jonarbi, who am I to tell you how to handle your own responsibility? Don't let their misfortunate fill your heart with guilt."

"Then there was another group of men, and some women asking for money, and they…"

"Do not let them trouble you, my love. All of them made their decision. If they had a chance to do better, they let the opportunity slip through their fingers."

"You are right."

"Why are you mentioning the poor? They do not have anything to do with us. We have money and our needs are met."

Jonarbi answered, "I am certain that I am making the best decisions with our money. I cannot afford to be careless. Sarah, our situation is improving but not as quickly as I would like."

"Your ambition is as far as the stars. Our children idolize you and want to be just like you when they grow up. I depend on you. If my father did not think much of you, Jonarbi, he would have never given you my hand in marriage. I remember him saying these words."

"Sarah, you are right."

"We are not going to be on the road begging. Please – do not worry. Our children will never want or be in need of anything. Nobody can do the things you do. I believe in you. You can either cast your cares away, or ask your father for money."

"I am not moving my family into my father's house. That is too much shame for any man to bear."

The two settled down for the night and the children went to their room. Jonarbi awoke late in the night. He got dressed quickly and gathered an empty sack with a tie at the opening and placed it within his cloak. Quietly he told his wife he loved her, and left the house.

He started to walk down the main roads and as he approached the larger building, he kept out of sight. Jonarbi broke into the back door. He searched through the room, but the treasury wasn't there so he checked another room. He knocked over a couple of items and made some noise. The chest that should be filled with money wasn't there either. After sifting through a third room, Jonarbi found the chest. He broke the lock and began to grab coins by the handful.

Jonarbi moved with urgency, but it was all in vain. Excluding my presence, there was a group of five men at the door watching Jonarbi from a distance in the hallway. When the thief made a noise, they treaded softly, but remained close enough to not cause a disturbance. The witnesses already knew the only way out of the room was through one door. When the men had seen enough, the man who held the lantern stepped forward, close to the entrance. Jonarbi was alarmed by the light.

Afraid of being caught, Jonarbi abandoned his quest for riches and suddenly ran. The first witness to the theft ran towards the man and lunged at him. Jonarbi took a step to the left and quickly took off to the right. With the first obstacle avoided, the robber continued his course. Jonarbi switched the coins from his right hand to his left hand to create space from the second witness. Although the man attempted to arrest Jonarbi, he used his free hand to strike the opposition in the chest.

I couldn't intervene in the escape or capture because I was not given permission by the Lord. Disasters must occur from time to time, and this was no exception. I could only write in my scroll, so I continued to write while Jonarbi did his best to escape. He anticipated when and where the next man could possibly hit him. As the man turned the corner through the door, a third witness ran towards his direction and closed in on his position.

Jonarbi saw him coming. He saw no other alternative, so he ran harder. The man who sought Jonarbi's capture pushed forward with his arms extended and the thief matched his efforts by lowering his shoulders for the encounter. Once the two met there was a struggle; one fought to advance in his escape, while the other strained muscles to bring his adversary to a halt. The advantage was temporarily the robber's as he kept his feet moving and shrugged off the counterattack. The third witness, however, was strengthened by the fourth man. With all of his might, the man leaped and collided with the robber. The attempt at larceny failed once Jonarbi fell to the ground.

The witnesses immediately took hold of the robber's arms, raised him to his feet and forced him against a wall. The first two witnesses met him and called him a robber, with much disgust. They threw blows at Jonarbi's face, slapping him with open palms. Jonarbi resisted the men and slipped one of his arms from being restrained. Jonarbi pushed one of the captors to the floor with his free arm. The robber pulled his other arm out of the man's grasp and pressed forward towards the door for his great escape. The men pulled on Jonarbi's robe but he kept pushing towards his mark. The fifth witness was dismayed by what he saw, and threw an astonishing blow to the chin of the criminal. Jonarbi rocked upon the heels of his feet and when he hit the floor, his eyes were closed.

"How wicked could a man be to do this? Bring this lost soul outside!" the well-dressed man ordered.

As soon as the men dragged Jonarbi's body outside, the men hurled their insults, ripped his robe, and spat on him. One of the witnesses had come forward and delivered a blow to Jonarbi's head while he was unconscious. The robber remained still, almost lifeless. A couple of the others checked his body to ensure he was still alive. So far, I had not touched the robber.

"Rabbi, what should we do with this jackal?" one of the witnesses asked.

The rabbi replied, "Go out and search for officials, quickly. They will see that he reaps the consequences of his actions."

The two went out into the city and returned with officials. The demons from earlier accompanied them. Jonarbi remained in a dream state. An official reached down and patted his face and shook him. The robber groaned showing he was still alive. The soldiers immediately kicked Jonarbi and brought him to his feet. Jonarbi was afraid and did not resist arrest. I knew that the Roman officials were not going to carry out a sentence at this time of hour, so my attention left this place. I then looked beyond the stars for my next assignment and had begun to ascend from earth.

As the soldiers proceeded to take him to jail, the dark shadows yelled at me, "We were right. Surely he will die. We have something great in store for him. You'll see."

CHAPTER THREE

While passing through the earth's atmosphere, I meditated over God's instructions. He wanted me to record what would happen during this trip to earth. Nothing seemed to be out of the ordinary to me. Yet once I returned to earth I realized that something was different. I couldn't put my finger on it at first. There was a heightened sense of things since I had left earlier that morning.

There was a man who appeared to be suffering from hunger and thirst. I assume that his belly had not been fully satisfied for a few days, if not a couple of weeks. He was close to madness and his gums were bleeding from extreme dryness. I had not received instructions to tend to this man, but I set my eyes on his actions. I watched him closely because I did not know if my plans would suddenly change. God is known for changing the plans from time to time so I remained focused. His body was skinny, frail, and dirty. His robe hung flat from his shoulders without much substance underneath. The way that the clothing fit him suggested that he was once bigger or the clothing given to him previously belonged to a much larger man.

The voice of my heavenly Father echoed when He told me to watch Kanaar. I made note of the man's name, and I observed some more. Many of his teeth were chipped, and quite a few were missing. My Lord spoke to give me some info about him. Poor Kanaar walked aimlessly from town to town, and city to city. As he sat on the road, pedestrians walked around him. They looked at him with no pity. The man had trouble with a limp and was unable to walk in a straight path. He didn't look like he was going to fight the good fight much longer. He looked as though he had dreamed that he would stay alive just long enough to see his last meal. On this cruel sunny day there wasn't an insect in sight to provide nourishment. Even so, he didn't look like he had enough strength or speed to catch one. As I looked closer, I saw that Kanaar had bumps that went from his head to his feet.

Kanaar suddenly exclaimed while looking towards the sky, "Why can't you grant me a better life? What have I done to dishonor you? I haven't done anything to deserve this! If you cannot help me you truly do not exist!"

Frustrated, he started to kick some rocks that were lying on the ground and parts of his feet began to ooze with puss and blood. I noticed that something else was amiss with this man. He was tormented by the evil spirit of envy. He felt alone. In spite of all of his ailments, he wasn't alone. Kanaar had one friend.

The other man was awakened by Kanaar's outburst, grumbling, "I should've expected you were complaining about something. I was having such a great dream until you started to groan."

"Ghapo, you don't understand my pain," Kanaar responded.

"We placed a similar rock under our heads to sleep on, Kanaar. Your possessions are small while mine are only a few. The spiders that crawl on you at night only do so after becoming bored of being on top of my idle body. Neither one of us has found shelter from God's scorn by giving us a disease which was no cause of our own. So tell me, what pains are you tied to this time that I have not dragged along?"

"Today was the day that the world turned its back on me."

"Kanaar, has it really been four years ago since this happened?"

"Yes. I have envisioned the same memory for four years. In the days leading up to it I felt like myself. I was completely normal and whole. I was in good health. All was well until I noticed a bump on my right leg. I should've taken my chance and cut off that leg."

"Kanaar, how would you have known that single bump would grow into this? No one in your family could have known. The doctors didn't know either."

"Unfortunately, this day haunts me and death has been tied to my back ever since. I'm tormented. I feel like I've had my last breath multiple times but it still hasn't come yet. I remember my mother and father taking me to one doctor, and another, and another. By that time the bump turned into a small patch that covered the back of my leg," Kanaar answered. "The next day it covered my entire leg and started to show on my other leg. Once they saw what was happening, my parents had become afraid of what a doctor would say to other people about me. More importantly, they were so afraid of what people would say about them and what could potentially spread to my brothers and sisters, that they made one swift decision."

"And this is why you are here? If this is so, you have to stop blaming your family. If I were in their shoes, I would've done the same."

Kanaar asked, "Would you lower yourself to their morals? Those cowards sent me where the untouchables live. I was only 13 years old then. My selfish parents gave me two days of clothing in a sack along with 10 shekels of silver. My mother didn't even bother to walk me to the front door. Four years later they are all prospering while I am waiting to die."

"Be grateful you have a memory of a loving family that is still alive. My parents and sisters did not take news of my illness well. Every one of them died, wishing I could get better. I tried to run away yet my family encouraged me to stay, *hoping* that my ailment would pass by. Now I've lost all of my family over something out of my control, yet I cannot get rid of the shame and guilt that came from this. I am overly confused sometimes, but I cannot take this out on my family because my parents didn't purposely give the burden to me. Your parents didn't give your ailments to you either. Be thankful for your good memories of them and surely you will make good ones in the future," Ghapo answered.

"I suppose."

"You are a true mystery. I am truly sorry that you rose to see the sunshine, again. Count your blessings, Kanaar."

Ghapo spoke with more reason, encouraging Kanaar that everything would be alright. Although the man didn't have much to his name, he made sure he brought his jar, and a small figurine. Kanaar looked upon it with great perplexity. The image of the idol was small enough to be hidden within his grasp, yet he knelt before it and revered to it as a holy thing. The misguided soul picked it up with both hands as if he were a young child carrying fragile pottery. He placed it within his cloak before they set their sights towards the city.

I watched them both closely, and I wondered if they would both die of malnutrition or some other disease. They both looked too weak to go on. The friend was in no better shape than Kanaar. He was slightly taller and had more front teeth than Kanaar, but that's about it. These two men were on the same journey of mere survival, from day to day. Sadly, they won't make it much further.

The two were now entering the city gates. They walked as if they were self-conscious about their conditions. They sauntered slowly with their head bowed, looking towards the ground at all times. They were allowed to roam into the city square; however, it was frowned upon since they were so sickly. Kanaar and Ghapo walked humbly into the city to find a suitable place to beg. They did not have a job or business because they were hideous, so this was the only way to gain any source of income.

They found a large gathering. There were men and women walking all through the place. They sat and held out their jars, and called out to those strolling by, asking for spare change. They had little luck, and daily their ailments worked against them. The people in this community generally lacked compassion for someone that they did not know. This was the spirit I felt while watching the townspeople.

The men would tell the beggars "no," "I'll pray for you," "go away," or grunt their dislike. The women did not say much of anything. Many of them would act as if they have heard nothing or look awfully hard past them, ignoring Ghapo and Kanaar all together. Sometimes I witnessed their strategy working; sometimes it would be a more dramatic response— the insults were heavier to carry and the blunt force of the rejection sank their morale lower and lower. The two men went at this for hours and hours and neither was afraid of rejection.

"How's it going for you today?" asked Kanaar.

"So far, I have received seven silver coins," Ghapo responded.

He stated his surprise, "Seven silver coins, that is more than what I received all last week. You're on a mountain top!"

"Yes, maybe so. Maybe soon I'll be able to purchase new sandals…or already worn sandals, you get my point. Nevertheless, they'll be new to me. Then I'll look good enough to beg from the rich."

The men had a quick laugh and decided to take a break to search for their next meal. As they walked, they took out the coins in their possession and counted them. I walked closely behind them and ascertained their relationship. They didn't seem to be in a rush to find food, and I was patiently waiting for them to drop. My left hand put away the holy scroll, anticipating that soon it would be my time to strike. They didn't stand a chance in living much longer. Ghapo had a terrible cough. He did his best to hide it from Kanaar, yet I saw his cloth in his hand. Blood that was forced from his mouth made a stain.

"I see her words are coming true for us—now that we have a god in our possession," the friend stated.

Kanaar replied, "I think you're losing your head for believing everything you hear. We are in the same situation now, as last week and the week before that, you fool. And another thing, how are you saying 'us' when you always have the most coins at week's end? How come your hand reading friend doesn't have enough wealth to go around? She seems to only have enough to go to who is paying her. Your god is small enough to fit in your hand and your god gives me nothing."

The man on my left only pulled out a couple silver quinarii, while the other pulled out a sack of silver quinarii and plenty of bronze sestertii and dupondii. They counted it all, and divided it evenly amongst themselves. They went to the marketplace and purchased soup together.

"Things are turning around for us, trust me, and don't I always share what I have with you? The dupondii in my hands is equal to what is in yours. Many times it never added up to one quinarii. But now, our empty palms have more money. The hand reader predicted this. I have full faith that good fortune and things will come to pass," replied the friend.

"Well I'm enlightened. Perhaps, the next time you see her and give her our food money, you should wash your hands before the ceremony begins. Maybe she can tell the future better. She will say 'Oh, I believe you will be hungrier than normal' you sloth," said Kanaar, while taking a gulp of soup.

"Today you aren't going to stir up anger. Besides, I have scheduled a meeting with her in a few days and she is looking forward to seeing me. All of this means I'll be alive to see it despite all odds."

"You aren't seeing the future any more than that drunken lady. I've joined you on one of those arranged visits, remember? You sat down with her and both of you overindulged in wine, which is a total coincidence since your god is the god of wine. Then the drunken fool stared at your hands, and started rubbing your palms and you agreed with everything she said. 'Oh my dear, your soul will witness a great peace of mind and you will be carefree. If you want more good news it will only cost one denarii for your next reading.' Put your idol to rest."

"You know, you talk down to your best friend about being hopeful, yet you don't have any motivation or peace to move forward with your own life at this moment. Since you have these dreams of Joseph that you seem to never share with me, why do you decide to wake up each day? What is life's secret? What is your solution for the madness?"

"My mind doesn't deal well with the sight of blood I guess. My stomach has always become ill when I see it. I'm afraid I'll see my own blood and get sick if I tried to kill myself. It doesn't make sense why a dying man is worried about feeling queasy but that's just me. Fate forces me to make the best choice out of a bad situation, and that's all there is to it."

"Yes and you're lucky to have a friend that has stopped you from trying out ways that wouldn't draw blood. Everyone needs *hope* Kanaar. Don't fight against everything that comes along your way."

"I'm not, Ghapo, but I need something *real*. Those three silver coins could've gotten us more soup so we can live. Real food in our stomach has substance. You spent it to listen to what a fortune teller had to say. We both would've been better off buying wine for ourselves, instead of entertaining someone who is full of wine, and full of dung. You are doing us both a disservice."

"You know me better than most so I'm going to say this gently to you: the notion that wrong is wrong and sin is sin is subjective."

"Subjective? You are screwing with both of our livelihoods. How is this subjective?"

"Yes, it is subjective. You think I've wronged you because I spent my own money on something that doesn't involve you. But, I helped pay for the food you are eating today—and you still have a negative opinion as if I've sinned against you. If I want to take heed to a hand reader for knowledge, that is alright with me and the Roman government. As long as that lady makes an income and pays her taxes, there is no wrong done. She has her ultimate leader she follows, and since I follow her there is no problem because no laws were broken. Our god, Bacchus, follows the laws of the land and he wouldn't break them. If I resided in a land where the government believed in no religion at all or one different than mine, it would be a sin to listen to the palm reader."

"That's the most foolish opinion I've ever heard."

"We can only be hopeful for better days despite the current circumstances we face or governments we live under, but there are no promises. None of us have ever seen God or any of the gods before so how do we know for sure? Surely the true God would show himself if He truly wanted to. We have just one life to live, and that's it. I mean I'm not judging, but look at you. Looking objectively at the way your life is, you're just as messed up as I am. You spend money that could've gone to food towards a 'good time.' Those prostitutes have a hold on you the same way I want to have the truth about life and how to live it, but it's against the law to be a prostitute. You are always around them, but you don't receive the same punishment as them because you aren't the one committing the sin."

"You have a point, especially about how I do not receive the same punishment as them. But you are wrong about the prostitutes. I don't love the whores for the sake of them being whores," Kanaar began to explain. "I only love the *thrill* of being with them. With them, I can fulfill desires

30

and pleasures and things I've never thought of. With my ailments I am unable to fulfill any of the good things in life I've always wanted to do. My mind craves an *escape* from this reality, the things I cannot control. I don't know another way that is as effective in making me feel *free*. The enemy has me trapped within these bones and skin all the time."

"Kanaar, I know that feeling. Even though I want knowledge to do what is right, I am not sure I'll ever have the *privilege* to command change into my life with all of these righteous living teachings. My circumstances related to my health won't allow it. Sometimes I wonder why I try so hard in the first place."

"Take this parable to heart since we are close to a predominant YHWH-worshipping community: I am a hardworking man with a wife and children. I love them so much, but this Jewish woman has caught my eye. She is a prostitute and for some reason I can't get her out of my head. Whether it's out of lust or some other impairment of judgment, I seek her and sleep with her. I pay my money and go about my way. Neither of us made an atonement of any sort. Now Ghapo, according to sin being subjective, who has sinned?"

"Nice one. Alright Kanaar, well you would have done wrong for committing adultery, and the woman has done wrong for living the life of a prostitute. However, you being a family man and part of the community, the rulers of both government and faith will give you a blind eye because on the outside looking in, who wouldn't want you to represent their god? Even though you paid a prostitute, you still serve YHWH and paid your ten percent tithe. In addition you pay taxes to the government, so the Romans and the Jewish community need you. Therefore, you will be generally considered not committing a sin. The woman, however, has nothing to offer or supply any means of support to giving money to the temple and she probably is not paying taxes to Caesar. Therefore, she is rightfully stoned for committing sin."

Kanaar was indignant. "So are you telling me that this family man receives no condemnation simply because he looks better in society than me, yet I'm still looked upon as vermin even though we both slept with the same whore?"

"You're just upset because you spent your spare change on some whore in the last city we visited and she wasn't as fun as the one you spent your money on before that. You truly are petty and you have no plan on how to move forward. At least what I get for my money has a lasting effect on my life. Your pleasure doesn't make it past two days on your heart. Is that why you are so angry?"

"I guess I'm angry because I imagine the next whore will look like the last whore who stole my money."

The men had a few more laughs, and got up to leave. Ghapo needed assistance getting up, so Kanaar reached down to grab his hand. They started off in search of a new place to beg, since midday had passed. After walking a while, they decided to take a rest on the outskirts of town. As they were enjoying their conversation, my Lord instructed me to take Ghapo. So I reached out for Kanaar's friend. He began coughing violently and harder than ever before. There was nothing that Kanaar could do but yell.

"Are you okay? Come on, don't give up. We got to stick this journey out. Don't give up on me. Fight through it. You can't leave me now!"

The voice of the Lord said, "Arise, Ghapo."

Ghapo was now in my presence. I told Kanaar's friend that he shouldn't be afraid but he still was surprised and shocked that things had happened so fast. After introducing myself, we headed off to see the Most High. The Father had me on a tight schedule, so I needed to move quickly. I wondered why I wasn't given the orders to take Kanaar instead.

As we headed to Heaven, Kanaar yelled loudly towards Ghapo's figurine of Bacchus, "Why didn't you work for him? He spoke about how great you were, you stupid idol! I wish he never met you or the hand reader that suggested keeping you around at all times. You've done nothing to help. God, wherever you are, how could you let this happen?"

When Ghapo and I arrived at the heavenly gates, I bowed and stated, "My Lord, we are ready to begin."

"Good, right on time. I have waited patiently to meet him. Are you alright, Ghapo?" God asked.

Ghapo looked high in the air well above the gates to see God's face. He was in amazement as we started to review his entire life. His actions, his thoughts, his intentions, and his secrets were revealed. Ghapo attempted to give the Lord his reasons, yet when God replayed similar events that reaped similar results, my heavenly Father's disposition remained the same. My Lord's eyes filled with rage toward the end, however, when his life showed Ghapo praising, worshipping and revering to the hand reader's small figurine as a god.

"I see. Ghapo, who is Bacchus, the one of whom you speak so passionately?" God asked.

"I didn't know what I was doing. Have mercy on me I cannot explain the things I have done I just did what…"

"Where is this Bacchus that you hold so dear? Is this where your *hope* came from? Why is it this lie doesn't stand by your side on your day of judgment?"

The man fell on his face as he petitioned, "My Lord! The true and living God have mercy on me."

"Gabriel, is he in the Book of Life?"

Gabriel, my closest brother, stood within the gate next to a large book. I could hear the pages turn. Ghapo didn't hear one page since he began to repent and praise. With my experience of completing these assignments, this is expected for men and women like Ghapo—but it is all for naught.

The pages stopped and Gabriel stated, "I searched for Ghapo, and he is *not* in the Book of Life."

"What does that mean?" Ghapo asked.

I looked to him and said, "It means your soul will not live."

"My creation does not know his Master and the Master does not know His creation. Depart from me!" the Lord commanded.

Ghapo exclaimed, "No!"

He got up and ran a few steps towards the gate yelling, "I'm sorry! Please forgive me, my Lord, my…"

Before he reached the gate, his arm was turned behind his back and my other hand put my sword under his chin. Ghapo kicked and squirmed and screamed as little children do but he couldn't get free from my grip. I carried him high in the air and flew far away, distant from the heavenly Father. I was headed to a place my God had never known. I ignored the man's protest as we journeyed farther and farther away.

When we reached the gates of Hades, I flew over the gate, far above the pit where his soul would be destroyed. Below, the giant waves of fire moved restlessly and untamed and many souls from before were drowning under the unbearable heat of the lake. The souls beneath the surface struggled to reach the top for air. Tormented by this false hope of relief, one of them pulled another one down to put themselves up. However, when one broke the surface to breathe, a soul competed against the raging fire to consume the air. The heat of the sweeping blaze belittled that of the sun. Unfortunately, this would be short lived, and they would soon be pulled down once again and the encircled events would never pass away. The sorrow was always present never to be accompanied with rest, peace, or love.

As we flew closer to the pit, I released my hold on Ghapo so he would fall into the miserable abode. However, the man made one last attempt to save himself. Being in denial of his fate, he clung onto my left foot to prevent himself from falling. My burden had finally become lighter when my right heel met the crown of his head.

CHAPTER FOUR

Once I returned to earth, I yelled at an evil spirit, "Leave Kanaar alone! Has he not suffered enough this hour?"

Kanaar did not respond to what I said. He didn't flinch at my sudden outburst. He kept walking and stumbling; he muttered and cursed out loud as tears ran down his face while evil creatures accompanied him. Kanaar's path was now led by anger, grief and despair.

One demon told me, "Back off! This man is free to do what he wants. Look at him, Kanaar is pathetic. Let him act according to what he pleases."

The demon to his right cosigned, "He will curse God and die, just watch him."

"Go about your business; this soul is ours," another proclaimed.

I wondered why this weak man was being attacked by Satan's top generals. What were they up to? I wanted to give him a way out of this mess. I asked the Lord to give him a memory of the last time he was at his wits end and God had shown him favor, enough to satisfy him another day. If only he had something strong to hold on to, he could believe in *hope*. Then, he would once again be reminded that God would never forsake him.

My Father's commands did not change, so I wouldn't take his life, but only watch it unravel. Before he could come to his senses, the demons showed Kanaar a few bugs. They all moved so fast that they took his mind off of mourning his friend. The devil knew the body could be easily distracted by anything exciting. Some bugs even crawled upon Kanaar. They had many legs and were fast. They provoked Kanaar and angered him. Dark creepy crawlers ran across the top of his sandals. The brown and red spotted ones ran circles around his shin and calf muscle just for sport.

He cried out in agony, not because the bugs were causing a lot of pain but out of shock at the sight of the unusually large bugs. They looked more fulfilling than usual; the insects had become so attractive and appetizing to his starved pupils. So Kanaar began using all of his strength and concentration to grab one of these critters. Wings and legs were nearly nipped by the withered fingers. Eventually the bugs stopped crawling on him, and moved away from him. This lured Kanaar back into the city. Because the people in this city had treated him poorly, his heart turned cold.

Kanaar uttered, "I'm going to catch one of these bugs to eat if it's the last thing I do."

I wondered why Kanaar couldn't simply stop and think. Although his friend had passed away, Ghapo had a small stack of coins. Why couldn't he go back and just take his money and use it for his benefit? Why did he forsake his inheritance? Meanwhile, he started to show more signs of vulnerability to the destructive beings in his midst. He took Ghapo's figurine from his pocket. He squeezed it tightly until it broke and crumbled. It originally appeared to be a shape of some person or a king. His eyes watered as the head and chest of the pagan statue caved in.

Kanaar said out loud, "Some god you turned out to be."

The demons did not care that he never paid homage to the false deity. As long as he didn't find the real God, their plans were in good shape.

They mocked and joked and harassed the man all over town. They brought more bugs to accompany his anger — creatures with large, humming wings. A fuzzy one with large wings flew right by his ears, gently brushing the tips against the lobes. Nevertheless, he attempted time and time again to catch one. The possibility was new, energizing, and enticing. He had put his faith into a crunchy and slimy delight. Bugs had distracted him from paying any attention to his surroundings.

The man grew tired from all of the running and chasing, and leaned against a tree as the sun set. Confused, Kanaar surveyed the area as he gasped for air. Then Satan himself appeared. He had been lurking behind other trees, patiently waiting for the right time to attack. Satan walked quietly and calmly up to Kanaar. Satan reached out and held one of the tree branches. A bug with wings and a hundred feet crawled out from his cloak onto the tree. The bug quickly advanced onto Kanaar, then into his robe, bit him on the stomach and flew away. In a swift motion he grabbed a rock that sat close by, and threw the rock at the bug. At last, Kanaar finally killed one.

Kanaar grumbled, "Now I wish I had something better to eat, anything but this."

He picked up half of the squished bug and ate it in one gulp. The other half of the body squirmed. He picked up the same rock and noticed that it had a sharp edge. The weight of the rock felt easy for him. It was as if it was a perfect fit for Kanaar to have this rock.

Suddenly, a sweet smell of relief hit his nose. He looked around to see what it could be. As his taste buds danced with the taste of legs and other bug parts, he knew this smell did not come from today's appetizer. Lulled by the aroma, Kanaar quickly followed his nose to see where this new joy would lead him. Knowing that he was a stranger in this land, he kept close to the shadows, the trees and the bushes. He drew closer and closer to a home near the center of the town.

Reaching the opening of the home, he could barely contain his excitement. Clinching his hands on the rock that he used to kill the large insect gave him confidence. He shook his head in an attempt to ignore the rush running through his veins and crouched so he would not be easily seen. He heard laughing and joyful noise. He heard the chuckles of two small children. Kanaar also heard the voice of a woman. To ensure his plan would go through he waited patiently. After a moment passed, he assured himself that a man was not present in the house. While crouching, he quickly moved over to the opening. He muttered something to himself while holding the rock. Kanaar was committed to taking this gamble and he had come too far to simply become a coward. The desperate man lunged through the opening of their home and quickly grabbed the woman. The woman screamed and the young boys did as well.

The hopeless man yelled, "Get down!"

Kanaar kicked one of the boys down that stood near him and covered the woman's mouth with his disease-ridden hand. The woman's voice reduced to a whimper once she felt the edge of the rock across her neck. The boys followed suit and became quiet.

He quickly told the boys, "She won't be hurt if you stay back."

The boys seemed sheltered and looked as though they had never been exposed to a language like this, but they got the gist of what he was trying to say. Kanaar knew he did not have a lot of time to take action so he walked towards their lovely spread with haste, all while holding the woman hostage. He noticed one of the boys was so scared that he wet himself.

He quickly told the little one, "You are ridiculous for ruining your clothes boy. Now listen, you wash your hands and put a large portion of your lamb and bread to the side. I want the portion to be even bigger than your father's."

Kanaar looked toward his right and told the other young boy, "Well don't just stand there. Get a clean cloth to wrap the food in."

The little boy cried hysterically, "Mama? Mama!"

"Hurry up or I will strike her down."

The boys continued to cry as they scrambled to get the man's meal ready to go. Although he didn't cause any vital damage, Kanaar scratched the woman's neck deep enough to draw blood. The woman maintained her composure, as the boys saw the blood running down from the middle of her neck. The boys made a large portion, even sacrificing some of their own in fear of the man's threat. I started to think that God wanted me to follow this man because someone here was going to die. The dark shadows were witnessing what was taking place. They had become boisterous at the fatherless household being taken over by a mad man. Their entertainment was at the family's expense, paid for by a sweet smelling delight.

Kanaar's cravings could now be satisfied with the meal. His mouth began to salivate and he could not help himself. The bread was made fresh over the flame not too long ago. The outside was a shade darker than gold, but the inside would be light and flaky. It would be the perfect complement to a slow roasted lamb. The lamb had to have been young because the boys were able to break off pieces of meat without using a blade. The meat fell right off the bone, just for his delight. He smelled the seasoning of the meat and stared at the boys as he held their mother hostage.

The older boy handed the sack that contained the thief's dinner. With haste, the crippled man snatched the sack while simultaneously shoving the woman down to the ground. The young boy started to cry in relief that he was leaving but the older boy attempted to impede his exit. The boy reached and took hold of the crippled man's garments. Kanaar grew too impatient and threw an elbow back at the boy. He collapsed to the ground after being struck in the neck. With his clumsy footing, Kanaar hurried as quickly as he could over to the bushes. He then stole away from the light into complete darkness. Kanaar attempted to conceal his identity by running with his body lower to the ground than usual. Now being out of the middle of the city, the trees provided much more shade and protection from being seen.

CHAPTER FIVE

While Kanaar was getting away, there were three men standing outside of a house talking to one another. From a distance, they saw a man in torn clothing hunkering down and moving sporadically amongst the trees. The men did not know who he was, but a couple of them commented on the clothes he wore. The third man commented on the sack that was in his hand. Suddenly, the men heard a faint outcry from small children, and instinctually ran towards the cry.

"Something is wrong!" one of the men shouted to the others.

The men sprinted a great distance and finally reached the home. At this point there were people walking towards the home but no one had reached the opening. The three men continued to run and press towards the door. Finally, they reached the home and cautiously walked inside.

They saw one small boy kneeling next to his mother, tending to her wounds. The woman was lying down, and the boy held scraps of cloth in his small fingers. As the boy cried and wrapped the cloth around the mother's hands the three men asked what happened. They were outraged by what they heard.

"Thank the heavens that your lives were spared. What did the man look like?" asked one of the men.

"He was tall and skinny. The man had dark hair with bad teeth. His sandals were beaten up. His clothes were old and torn in certain places," replied the boy.

The older boy added, "He was starving. He didn't do any of this for money. He threw an elbow to my throat to get away when I tried to stop him."

The men started to look closer at the older child. They asked for the boy to move his hand off of his neck for a moment. They were angry at what they saw. A bruise so large on a small boy they thought that the man was a ruthless, conniving bastard, and demon-possessed. The boy was not even old enough to lie with a woman, let alone had the strength to defend himself.

The older boy, Julius, stated, "He made me give him my father's portion of food. He took our lamb and bread. When my brother gave it to him I tried to get in his way. I tried to stop him. I tried."

The two boys and the three men began to focus their eyes on the woman lying down. She looked to be in a daze. With slight confusion she asked what has happened. Her hands were bruised due to the impact she had with the bare ground. Her son attempted to aid the wound by wrapping them in a cloth. Blood still trickled from her neck yet the clotting began. Like her son, her head had a similar bruise located by her temple, but hers was noticeably swollen.

I did not want to leave the woman. She had suffered deeply when Kanaar robbed them of their evening supper. I could not believe that I once took pity on Kanaar. I felt that this monster deserved to see justice served whatever that might be. I only remained calm due to the aid that had been rendered. The two boys had done the best that they could and the men were available to give their assistance when needed.

The woman whimpered, "My head hurts so bad and I'm thirsty. Can you please bring me some water?"

"Young child, please bring your mother some water."

Julius went over to where the food was being held in their home. He located a jar that contained some water and one that contained vinegar. He brought both jars over to where his mother lay. She first took a drink of the water. One of the three men soaked the cloth with vinegar and applied it to her head. After that, Julius wiped her neck. The mother made small chatter, and she told them everything that she remembered about what happened. The men did not say a word. They, too, were astonished as to what has happened and took pity on her.

One of the men asked her, "What is your name?"

She answered, "My name is Kiyah."

The men followed suit and introduced themselves, also exchanging names with the boys. They asked for her blessing to stick around for a while, fearing that the man would return during the same night for more food. They anticipated a desperate man would make a return, even after she and her boys were screaming so loud that no one could go without notice. Kiyah gave them her blessing to stay in her home during the evening. She looked over at the food and was even more disheartened. She started to become overwhelmed with emotions of what has happened and began to cry.

The three men asked simultaneously:

"What's the matter?"

"Are you alright?"

"You still have some bread and meat over there. Are you hungry?"

She only answered the last question, so the boys brought her over a piece of meat and bread. She apologized to the men for her home to look as it did, even though it was the robber that made a mess of everything. With slightly lifted spirits, she began looking over her shoulder and around the room. Kiyah grew anxious and paranoid over the man with torn clothes. The boys took notice of this and they both sat closely on both sides. She held them close in her arms for comfort.

Kiyah started to think out loud and stated, "I wonder when he will return."

"Who will return?"

"My husband."

The three men looked at each other. At first, they wondered how this home would appear to a man coming home from a hard day's work. A beaten wife and children did not look like all was well, especially when there were three men who remain in normal physical condition. The men made her promise that if they stayed, they would not be falsely accused of doing any wrongful act. Any man would be furious and would want to wreak havoc on anyone who may have looked like they played a role in the events that had taken place. Considering their position, she requested the men to help her move near the front door. Two of the men lifted Kiyah to her feet and walked her towards the front door. The other man placed his hands on the boys' shoulders as he walked, so they would be reassured that everything would be alright.

As they waited, God gave me another task for later in the night. Before leaving, the Most High instructed me to remain in the woman's home to keep a close eye on things. Kiyah seemed to be in better spirits. The three men and the family grew hungry. Out of respect for the father of the household, the family patiently waited for his arrival.

Suddenly the front door opened, and a large man entered the home. The three men were on high alert, but the woman was at peace along with the boys. The boys yelled in excitement that their father was finally home and ran to the door. Julius grabbed hold of one of the father's arms. The younger boy jumped into his chest, and held on to his father with all the strength that he had in him. The man was glad to be home, yet tired after a long day's work.

Oblivious to what had just happened, the man returned the embrace. "Boys, boys! It is good to see you. Where is your mother?"

The younger boy answered, "She's lying down over there. She needs her rest. A thief took our food and knocked him and mother to the ground."

"What did you say?"

"The man was mean and somehow entered our door. He grabbed mother and made demands for our meal this evening. He took *your* share of food and ran off."

The large man had heard enough of this. With haste he closed the front door behind him. He put his youngest son on the ground and looked into Kiyah's eyes with disbelief. He called out her name and she replied. He walked towards Kiyah and drew his sword from his side. He saw three men standing around her while she was lying on the ground. He was full of rage. The men were full of dread and fear, so they collapsed and fell to their knees.

"Please do not strike your servants. Please don't kill us," the men shouted.

As the large man slowed his sprint to a walk, he responded, "Why shouldn't I? Who are you and why are you in my home? Do you know who she is, or who I am? Your presence alone has truly sealed your doom!"

The men pleaded, as their good deed was now being punished. The large hand of the homeowner raised his sharp and shiny sword in the air with mal-intent. Surely one, if not two of the men were certainly going to taste death soon. Yet while he raised his hand, something peculiar happened right before his eyes. The woman mustered enough strength in her body to throw herself before the men. She was already on the floor but she dove from her knees towards her husband. She looked him directly into his eyes and reached towards him helplessly.

Kiyah screamed, "Lucretius stop!"

Slowing down the motion of his arms he asked, "Who are these men?"

She explained, "These men came to our help after we were robbed. There was a bony, desperate man with wild hair that barged into our home. Somehow he came through the front door without breaking it. He held me hostage and demanded the boys make him supper. The bandit told them to make his food in the same size portion as if they were making a plate for their father. I assumed he thought they were helpless children since you were not here to defend us."

Lucretius put his sword away. Although still skeptical of the situation at hand, he reached out to the men to take hold of their forearms and helped the men up to their feet. The large man stood higher than the other three men, and was draped in the royal red and bronze. His eyes were cold blue as he looked upon them. He reserved his heart and peace only for his family. There were veins bulging around his temples, down his neck, and all throughout his body. His pale skin was guarded by the calluses on his palms, his Roman Empire attire, his helmet, and breastplate. Even though he wanted to attack, his wife's voice put him somewhat at ease. Otherwise, I am confident I would have been making another voyage to the Father soon.

Soon after his wife explained in full detail all of what had happened and the men told where their story began, the centurion decided to take immediate action. After the men left the house, Lucretius gathered his top soldiers for the man hunt. They went from house to house. Lucretius was determined to find the thief tonight. His rage flowed effortlessly throughout his body. He had a new vigor in his step in this late hour. It was infectious. The soldiers had been put off that the centurion was approaching them at that time of night, but they were outraged by what they heard.

I have seen many men that stood for justice and for the law instantly want justice to be served if their loved ones are involved. Lucretius' men were ready to go. Blood ran through their veins to shed the blood of others. It was in their power to carry out their desires, and the three witnesses knew the intentions of the soldiers as if it were written on their foreheads.

CHAPTER SIX

After walking around, the men gathered in the center of the city. Lucretius stood amongst the large soldiers. All were standing at attention, focused on their leader's next move. The general walked back and forth, back and forth, searching for the words to explain the extent of his disgust. The men were tightly arranged in a half circle around the centurion. They were militant and anxious, as they awaited their orders.

He then started to speak with a sharp tone, "I feel a great pain in my head and my side, from what these three men have seen. These men were helping my wife and my boys in my absence. I almost killed them out of haste, not knowing why they were in my home. My wife was struck around her head and neck, my boys likewise. Rome's wife and Rome's sons were struck by no fault of their own. This traitor against Rome that we will search for tonight could've gotten into any of our homes for any reason and harmed our defenseless ones that we cherish the most. This man robbed me of *my* food, and ran off and thought there would be no consequences for his actions. What a coward! Surely any man would be troubled, but my family is *our own*, so he is no better than a traitor against Caesar."

The familiar dark shadows that were mocking and belittling Kanaar, now deliberately chose to take advantage of the surrounding soldiers. Since

Lucretius was a high-ranking official it was in his authority to arrest a criminal. The dark shadows close by had influenced him with hate. His trusted men kept each other's hearts filled with hate. I was thinking that the poor Kanaar would not see tomorrow morning if these men found him anytime soon. I could not say when Lucretius planned on killing Kanaar, but I did witness how quick he was to draw his sword.

The leader told the others, "We will split up. We must get him. I must get him! These three men have seen this cursed soul with their own eyes. They will give you the visual to keep you on track. Unless he attempts to resist arrest, no one is to use excessive force. Leave that to me. Let's split up and move out. We will meet back here in three hours. This son of a jackal couldn't have moved far."

God's voice told me to catch up with Kanaar, so I left the assembly of the soldiers. The man sat against a tree in the outskirts of the city. His mouth begged for the tender roast and the fresh baked bread. Kanaar was weak and begged for nourishment. He quickly reached for his sack of food and hastily tried to unwrap his meal. He would've eaten the scrap of cloth that covered his meal if he could've. The first few bites of bread he inhaled and didn't let himself taste or savor it. Overwhelmed by the thought of a satisfying mouthful for so long, finally he received his reward in full. He took a huge bite of the glorious lamb. It was seasoned to perfection; a flavorful dry rub had been used in the preparation. He tasted the savory meat along with a hint of spice. It was a delightful smell even to me. The lamb was still warm. He enjoyed his meal — this time he ate without revering to anyone. For god did not make a way for this meal to happen, Kanaar made a way all on his own. The torment of eating bugs for mere survival had taken a toll on his spirit, but tonight he dined and he was paid in full.

Kanaar said out loud to himself, "This is good. I have to slow down though."

His stomach was not used to eating such rich food and he wasn't used to the size of the meal. He randomly thought of how it compared to his daily size that has preserved his life up to this point. It was blasphemous to thank God or anyone's god for that matter. He was confused about what to think of the whole matter now that he had the sweet victory in his hands. Kanaar began to think hard for a moment. He had a perplexed gaze on his face while he looked into the darkness before him.

He wanted to get up and walk just for a few more steps to get further outside of the city. There is a spot where untouchables went to sleep, and stored some of the few belongings that they've kept. He had a change of clothes and he also had some shreds of cloth to keep him warm during the night's rest there. The demons knew this. Even though his eyes were focused on the darkness and restarting his walk to go further into the darkness, the darkness focused his ears on the rumbling of his stomach. Kanaar decided to sit back down and eat more of the food in the sack. There was so much good food there that the skinny man found an extra cut of lamb, a piece that he was overjoyed to see. As one single tear fell down his face, he ate and savored the last piece of meat.

There was no more meat or bread to consume at that point. The demons were laughing with one another and decided he was doomed. Their mission was accomplished and they started to walk away. The man was not used to eating rich food. You could tell by looking at him! You could barely pinch the skin on his arm he was so thin. He looked foolish as he sat there, being a glutton. He was barely aware of anything, and the wind and the sounds of the uncertain nighttime now played a lullaby for Kanaar. He was food drunk. He was deeply satisfied with his meal and although he knew that he probably should relocate, he didn't budge a cubit. He sat there and let his eyes roll to the back of his head and his eyelids slowly closed thereafter.

Later on that night, Kanaar was awakened by the feeling of eyes watching him. As quickly as possible the man started to crawl, and while hunched over, he began to run. Unfortunately, one of the smaller men that saw him in the woods confirmed that this was the man who committed the crime. The men were within an arrow shot and were already closing in on his position. Kanaar stubbornly ran left and saw a soldier — ran right and saw another. His joy was now long gone, just like the dinner he had. One of the guards dove and tackled him. The other two guards ran over to help pin him to the ground. I watched in awe how skilled these men were. There was no chance that Kanaar was going to get away.

"Great execution, men," Lucretius' second in command, Aquila, stated. "What is your name?" he asked Kanaar.

Reluctant to give his name, he replied, "What is this all for?"

After a guard slapped him across the face and jammed his foot into his toes, Kanaar yelled, "Aww! I didn't do anything!"

The guard closest to him became quite irritated by his replies. In one flowing, sweeping motion, he slammed Kanaar back down to the ground and drew his sword. To establish dominance, he forced Kanaar's face into the dirt and animal droppings. The soldier put his blade close to Kanaar's temple and leaned in close.

"I do not have time to interrogate, for the one who sends us is blood-drunk. It is in your best interest that you tell me your name so you will not anger him any further. You can have a lighter load if you comply so let go of your arrogance. Now tell me your name!"

Still in shock of what was happening, Kanaar couldn't utter a word. Although the guards became furious with the man's insubordination, the men had strict orders not to strike the man until they brought him back to the meeting grounds. They knew under these circumstances that it would be best to follow orders. The man yelled curses at him and grunted in frustration. The soldier put away his sword and lifted the skinny man back up to his feet. The other soldier brought over chains and shackles. They wrapped Kanaar's body, linking his arms to his waist and his waist to his feet.

While doing so, the witness asked, "Can me and my fellow friends be released now? For you remember that we have not done anything wrong and..."

"No. You are not released until our leader says so. We all must return to meet in the city. Only then will you be released. Understood?" Aquila asked.

The witness nodded and looked Kanaar directly into his eyes. The informant had some relief that he wasn't the one being arrested, for Kanaar did not know the extent of the trouble he'd gotten himself into. Lucretius' source was glad that he was closer to being freed from duty, and wasn't concerned about what was going to happen to Kanaar.

I looked towards heaven, towards my heavenly Father. In the darkness of the night I did not want to lose my focus. I wanted to seek direction in what I am supposed to do. I closed my eyes and hoped for Kanaar's sake that the men would do whatever they must in a quick efficient fashion so his pain wouldn't linger. However, the Planner had something different in mind. I was instructed to follow him for now. I opened my eyes and began to follow the soldiers back to the inner city.

Once the men arrived to meet with the centurion and the other soldiers, I started to believe my duties were going to pick up soon. Kanaar was doomed. The leader looked upon him with deep feelings of anger and hate. Lucretius couldn't stand still. Once again he paced back and forth, back and forth, and then he went from left to right. He finally slowed down and began to speak.

"You three come forth," the centurion ordered as three men stood next to each other.

As they walked towards the center of the group he continued, "I have heard all of your accounts of what happened, in addition to my wife and sons' accounts of what has happened. You all have given a description of the man who committed this crime. Does this man fit your description?"

"Yes," answered the men.

"Does this man look like the running and wandering man in your memory?"

"Yes."

Aquila stated, "He should be subject to the full extent of the law. This fool at this moment thinks he's better than the law and won't answer simple questions from soldiers."

"Yes, that is a great problem indeed. What do you think?" Lucretius asked.

The informant who identified Kanaar exclaimed, "This man is doomed and he will burn. He lost the right to everything when he committed this crime, especially against your family. You are a gracious man considering he is still alive!"

"Hmmmm, you all bring up great points. Because of the law, we are already committed to delivering a just punishment but I am always interested in hearing our citizens' opinion. Well then, your work is all done for tonight and for this entire matter. You may retire and go home."

The three men bowed before Lucretius and quickly left. The commander started walking toward Kanaar. The demons were back, and in larger numbers. They walked amongst the soldiers. Now there was violent shoving, spitting, and slapping the criminal across his face. One of the dark shadows walked over to Lucretius and Aquila. He started to taint their fair judgment towards the criminal. The demon taunted the Roman leaders' logic and responsible actions.

He said terrible and awful things as to what he should do to the criminal right now. I began to speak to the soldier as well. I tried to tell him the battle is already won, why give in to such level of hate. To dishonor his wife and kids in this matter would be a terrible mistake. On the walk to the prison, the leader made up his mind. He tapped his second in command on the shoulder and looked towards the right. There was a small secluded area amongst the trees and bushes. Although they were in the middle of the city, at this time of night it was hidden by darkness and out of plain sight.

As he tilted his head toward that area, Lucretius asked his lieutenant, "What do you think of that area?"

Aquila replied, "That would be a great area to exact justice. He harmed your family, your judgment is correct but it doesn't quench your thirst for blood. You have to set the record straight with this thief. Even the informant said he needs to be judged to the full extent of the law."

"He did say that, didn't he?" the centurion stated with a tone of relief.

They both laughed and agreed on what was going to happen without saying any further words. They all began to walk towards the small brush of bushes, trees and grass. Kanaar trembled with fear of what was about to happen. The centurion looked anxious, and he overheard the one soldier say the words "get him." That could mean anything was bound to happen, hell could temporarily reign on earth in Kanaar's eyes.

Once the soldiers reached the small area, Lucretius ordered, "Release him."

The leader suddenly hit Kanaar across the neck with a blistering speed. His feet left the ground as he was struck. Once he fell, a few soldiers kicked him and another one stepped on Kanaar's hand. When the wind was temporarily knocked out of him, the soldiers proceeded to unlock the chains that kept him bound.

The large man then stated, "Get up and state your name."

Kanaar squirmed on the ground and a soldier that stood by started to whip him with the very chains that had kept him bound. Kanaar yelled in agony. He struggled and finally brought himself to his feet, but the soldiers continued to push him back and forth.

The centurion raised his hand while saying, "What is your name?"

The soldiers stopped shoving him to give him a chance to answer. Kanaar was shaken from the beating that he had received, but still had a perplexed look on his face. He just stood there, with his left hand balled up in a fist. Out of nervousness he stood and waited to calm down.

"I'm going to ask one last time— what is your name?" asked Lucretius.

"Kanaar."

"Alright Kanaar. Do you understand what the three men and my family are accusing you of?"

"No I do not. What am I accused of?"

The demons were egging Lucretius on, twisting the meaning behind the words. The leader was going to strike Kanaar at any moment. He didn't have any reason to hold back. Kanaar was playing with his emotions and he candidly gave insulting answers to his questions. I even admit I haven't seen a dying man act in this manner in a long time. It's as if he had nothing to lose, and looking at his predicament, he didn't expect to live to see tomorrow. I didn't see it either, but God's orders have not changed.

After regaining some of his composure, the centurion said, "You are accused of robbery. You are said to have held my wife hostage for food and struck her and my young boys in the process. Three men identified you as the man who robbed my home. In my eyes you are guilty but there's something missing."

"What do you mean?"

"Well you see, I have witnesses that saw you running away, which matches the boys and my wife's description, but my family said you ordered them to give you MY portion of food, but I do not see you holding anything. So, how was it?"

"I don't have any food."

"Of course you don't have it. You ate it!"

He lunged at Kanaar with all the speed and strength in his body. He swung his right hand close under the sternum, where the stomach sits. He hit him so hard Kanaar instantly threw up. Food and stomach acid flew from his mouth into the ground and onto Lucretius' right arm.

"Ah! Here's the proof. Doesn't this look familiar to you, Kanaar?"

"Yes, I remember," he said painfully.

"So you do remember eating the food I was supposed to eat?"

"Yes."

Lucretius began punching the criminal in the face, knocking out one of Kanaar's few teeth. The other soldiers jeered at the criminal as they circled around him. The centurion took a break from beating him to wipe off his arm with the spare cloth he had brought along with him during this manhunt. The other soldiers began to whip the criminal with the chains and shackles once again. The criminal yelled in pain. The leader of the group was fed up with the sight of Kanaar at this point. One of the soldiers was going to help get Kanaar back on his feet and reached down for his arm. Kanaar immediately blocked his hand and pushed the soldier away. This angered the guard and so the Roman lunged at him with a fist. Kanaar dodged the fist and was able to lay a blow of his own. Kanaar was shocked that his left fist connected with the guard. He swung like a wild man.

Another guard tackled Kanaar and forced him to the ground. Somehow Kanaar was able to struggle to get out of the soldier's hold and reached for his rock from earlier. He had been holding on to it the entire time and dropped it when the general knocked the dinner out of his system. He grabbed hold of the rock when two other guards started to repeatedly kick him in the stomach. They kicked him until Kanaar showed little resistance. Once he was still, beaten, and out of breath, the soldiers got Kanaar back on his feet. The demons were curious about what was going to happen, because they knew the poor fellow had gone mad and didn't have any morals or standards of conduct at this point. The criminal somehow mustered enough strength to push a guard out of arms reach and swung his right hand. He hit the soldier in a way that he didn't expect.

"This jackal cut me. He has drawn blood!" one of the soldiers shouted.

The other soldiers were shocked to hear that a criminal, a pathetic skinny man had enough nerve and the stones to strike a Roman official. The spirits from under were screaming "kill him" over and over. The attacked soldier tackled Kanaar out of frustration and threw him to the ground, then punched him mercilessly until there wasn't much movement in his body. Then, the same soldier forced Kanaar back on his feet again to stand accountable.

The man in charge examined the soldier who had been attacked and said, "You did not tell a lie. Kanaar, this will cost you, greatly."

He signaled for four of the guards to beat him down once more. The beating continued for a short period. Then the general raised his hand. The beating stopped and they put Kanaar back on his feet. The commander looked upon Kanaar still filled with hate.

"Is that how you hit my wife, and my boys?"

The air was knocked out of the criminal, and he wasn't able to answer the question quickly. The centurion punched Kanaar once again in the gut. Kanaar didn't vomit this time because he didn't have anything else to give, but he started to dry heave and struggled to catch his breath. The punch was disabling and he dropped the rock he held. Another punch and Kanaar fell to his knees.

"This is for MY peace of mind!"

"Ahhhhh-ellllllllllll-aaaa! Aahhhhh!"

Even the other guards cringed a little bit. The centurion took hold of the back of his elbow and his wrist. With all the force he had in his body, he lifted and threw his knee once into Kanaar's forearm and he screamed. Yet Lucretius was not satisfied. His anger gave him a new mission and purpose. So, when he put his right foot back on the ground he had one thing on his mind: get him. He struck with his knee and broke Kanaar's arm. Being able to look through skin I saw the damage inflicted. One of the bones in the forearms was broken, while the other bone was completely shattered at a point between the elbow and wrist. The surrounding guards saw one of the bones now bulging awkwardly under the skin. Other bones have broken through the skin. The shadowy crowd was delighted. They jeered for more blood. The centurion decided to punch him a few times while Kanaar was defenseless wailing on the ground.

The Roman officer finally decided he was satisfied in what he saw and stopped. Lucretius was no longer thirsty for blood and revenge. His eyes didn't blink so he saw that despair, fear, and hopelessness surrounded Kanaar. Then he ordered his men to take him into the prison and then retire for the night. Being cognizant of Pontius Pilate, however, Lucretius knew he had made a mistake. Pontius Pilate grew tired of the criminals being severely beaten before they were formally charged under his rule. Therefore, the centurion decided to dress up the situation.

He ordered one of the men to bring a pitcher of water, a jar of vinegar, and a fresh clean cloth. Once the man returned he ordered that Kanaar wash his face and rinse his mouth of the excess blood. Kanaar complied. He then was ordered to take a few swallows of vinegar. Then Kanaar was given orders that he did not understand, at first. The leader did not want to cause a scene, so he told the criminal to bite down on the cloth.

Kanaar wanted to stop the pain so he followed instructions. He bit down on the folded cloth even though his mouth was severely sore and full of aches. The leader quickly whistled and three men forced him to the ground, on his back. From that point some men took hold of his arms out to his side and the others took hold of his ankle. Once the body was in place they looked towards the head of the group for further instruction.

"Kanaar bite down. You, straighten the arm."

A guard that stood nearby did the honors. He walked over and stepped on the arm. The point where there was an irregular shape and bulge was now under his feet. As he started to put his full body weight on his arm, Kanaar started to scream in pain. The criminal attempted to move but he couldn't. Then, the guard observed his work; he didn't do enough justice, so he started stomping the arm until the bone was forced somewhat back in normal form. Kanaar couldn't take the torment anymore for the evening, and passed out in shock.

After the brief flurry of hits, the leader deemed that the arm overall looked more swollen than before. The arm looked more swollen than irregular, which was a more favorable appearance. The men then put the shackles on the robber and dragged his now unconscious body towards the prison. I am not certain as to why I was asked to view all of this, since Kanaar was still in fact alive. After the men headed out, I was relieved to carry out other work. I left this city for one suitable for a horse and chariot to travel to. My Lord instructed me to arrange a meeting for Him in a couple of hours with a lady struck with high feverish symptoms.

CHAPTER SEVEN

After making a few other visits on Thursday, I received instructions to watch Yahshua. He is the Christ. He can do whatever He wants to do. Surely He has everything under control, at least more control than the thieves I was asked to watch. I didn't understand. Meanwhile, the devil wasted no time to find his earthly accomplices. A gathering of Jewish and Roman authorities now joined one of Christ's own, Judas.

After eating His supper with His twelve disciples, Yahshua knew the hour had drawn near. He asked Peter and Simon to watch him as He prayed. I prayed that my heavenly Father would reveal why I was here. Even though it is ludicrous that He would fall within my assignments, the one above wanted me to follow His footsteps. Yahshua controls life and death over himself not me, but He wants me to watch him.

This garden looked and felt just as profound as the Garden of Eden, but currently more significant. There were many of my brothers around, watching Yahshua, cheering Him on and praising Him. They were focused. Unfortunately, the fallen angels are still energized and ready to attempt to break His earthly physical will. Hostility filled the air. A brawl was brewing and stirring up similar to when God gave us the orders to kick Satan out of heaven. They were shouting threats and messages of fear at the top of their lungs; meanwhile my brothers cheered on our leader. The angels took guard and kept the gloomy spirits away from Him. Christ's physical body had become weak, and sweaty. He appeared to be heavy-hearted about all the things occurring in the garden and what would happen tonight.

Christ was the only human body in the middle of it all. The only one close to Christ was the prince of darkness. I could see why he asked God to grant him permission to test Yahshua because if it were up to my brothers, he would've been struck with twenty swords by now. There were a couple hundred of these demons out here. We weren't worried, because we were deep in numbers too. The crafty serpent looked strained, which was normal, but I had never seen Christ look like this. In the midst of it all, I saw my fellow commander, walking and encouraging the others to hold their ground. I flew over to speak with Gabriel.

"Gabriel, when did all of this happen?"

"When Satan opened his mouth, he knew Yahshua would be alone where no men were around to distract him, so he decided to fill that void."

"He knows whatever Christ says will come true. He simply wants to give all of those in God's kingdom hell and grief."

"I think the devil is trying to deter Christ from saying and confirming God's will with the words of his mouth," Gabriel said. "The devil has seen too many times that nothing is impossible for God. So he is using disturbances and the worldly senses to create weakness and fear."

"Indeed. My good friend, I have to ask you a question. Something is laid heavily on my heart. Our Father has given me orders but I do not understand why they were given to me. I've been assigned to watch two men closely but have yet to receive the orders to take their lives. You know that I stand firm on completing my tasks and transporting these souls to God as He has tasked me to do. I want a good report for my spiritual gift, but God will not allow me to finish my work. Isn't this kind of strange?" I asked.

"Hmmmm that is strange. You are the angel of death. For some reason He doesn't want you to draw your sword even though you're in arm's reach. That is interesting. Yet I honestly know from experience that following commands is better for your head than thinking you're the captain of the ship! That can cause a huge headache, and none of us can think as big, as wide, or as far in the future compared to God. There's no need to give ourselves that sort of trouble."

"I understand what you are saying. However, would I be lying to myself if I didn't acknowledge this conflict? These people are on my list because they are going to die, plain and simple. Why does God mention them to me but He does not want me to strike when I'm standing next to them? I would become irritated if I was a farmer who sowed seeds, and the rain came, but the crops did not come. It would be as if this yoke were chains wrapped around my body, holding me back. It is greatly discomforting."

"I understand what you mean."

"I know that the great I AM holds the earth and everything therein in His hands. Yet, I'm still being kept away from doing the work I've once done. I'm aching with disappointment. I trust God with all I have, but have you ever felt that this trust wasn't enough? What do I do now since God has yet to reveal His plan?"

"I walked in your sandals before, so I know the last thing you need to hear is an excuse to sing a song full of sorrow. I would continue to trust Him in all that He has to say. You have come so far knowing Him and believing Him, maybe He simply wants to test how far you can hold on to that same trust and belief, even though nothing makes sense right now. Being an angel or a human being, could you really fathom or be able to mentally grasp and take in all of the grandest highs and depths of God? Who can outthink God or truly understand why He is the way He is? He gives us the opportunity to hear His answers by giving us life itself, but we have the shortest memory and cannot hold on to them. Did you create the heavens and the earth with your voice?"

"No."

"God knows that you are in a mental bind, so continue to pursue Him. Look in the distance in front of you. Can't you see Christ is going through something? He doesn't look comfortable to me. Unfortunately, none of us can carry the weight for Him. There is absolutely nothing that we can do but stand tall in alliance. Surely, if the Messiah is going through something while He's on earth, there won't be any exception for anybody who is in His kingdom. When you are experiencing these troubles while being obedient to the Planner's steps, I'd say you are on the right track."

"Thank you for your words, Gabriel. I will continue to trust God blindly with my future steps."

"Surely when you have passed the test, you will understand the entire situation better, and you'll be more like Yahshua. Keep moving forward."

"Will do. I must go now."

But Gabriel stopped me and said, "It's peculiar that you, the angel of death, have feelings in the first place, never mind feeling *this* way. I have been told that I should keep three angels on standby. I didn't understand why, but I'm seeing the vision now. These angels weren't doing their normal tasks either, but because they followed God's command, they are available to assist you in your predicament. Take them along with you — for your protection tonight. I have a feeling something grand is going to happen, and we cannot allow anything to go awry. You will need them in order to fulfill God's word. Remember, you are not to interfere with Satan's plan, for he was given permission by God to test Christ. Since he did not ask God for any other demon to come close, God has only allowed him to get near Christ. Please continue to follow God's command and attend to everyone on your list."

I nodded and began to walk to the center of the garden. Demons were yelling and shouting in a way that they spat when they spoke. Demons attempted to get in my path. One approached me from my right. An angel quickly flew in, blocked his path and shoved him backwards. Then there was a cluster of angels and demons ahead of me, so I had to move slightly to the left. As I walked, the path cleared until a demon lunged at me from high in the air. As he came close, one of my brothers flapped his wings to meet him. He led his high flying attack with his shoulder and knocked the cursed spirit out of course. As I finally reached where Yahshua was praying, the last angel remained somewhat close, watching my back. He paced back and forth and randomly changed directions, to ensure that I would not be disturbed.

I humbly walked close enough to hear what was being said. I knew Yahshua felt my presence, and I did not want to come in between what Yahshua needed to accomplish that night. Yahshua looked weak yet determined to do what God had sent Him here to do. I recognized that agonizing look. I could relate to that look. It's how I felt the past few hours. It's a strange mixture of pain, exhaustion, and the conflicting feeling of knowing you can do something else to get out of the situation—yet you're not easily moved. Meanwhile, Satan was being a persistent adversary.

Satan told Yahshua, "Take it from me; the world is too large to change. I've been wreaking havoc all over the earth since before you were born to your mother. I've known how this world works since its beginning and that's all that matters—how the world works down here. How are you going to be influential and persuasive? These men and women are selfish and petty. A sister will not help her sister, brother, mother or father with something they need if it means forfeiting what she wants. That is what they know and hold on to. These people are too simple while your law is too complicated."

Yahshua looked heaven bound, "I come to show the world how to look towards the true God in heaven, for He will provide the things they need and the desires of their heart. They have seen me and will continue to learn how to love one another as they would love themselves."

"They won't listen to you. Your efforts are futile. They hate you. They are concerned with the here and now, none of that life after death nonsense. Surely they will die and be buried one day, and that is all. You should read more about the agnostic men. They got it all covered. It's ironic that the agnostic and other non-believers will bury the Son of God if you keep following God's will. Wouldn't you agree Yahshua? They will roll a bolder in place to seal in your lifeless body. Why would you go through all of that just to die and never come back? People could have lived their whole life ignorant of what you have to offer and died peacefully, and be in the same situation that you will be in—dead, rotting, and soon forgotten."

"Well, you never were an optimist. What good can possibly come from you?"

"You bring people back from the dead. I dare to ask, who is going to bring you back to life — one of the twelve disciples? Let me guess…will it be Judas, the one you called out at the dinner table? Since you believe in the power of life and death, shouldn't I kill all of your precious disciples? Then, who would come to save you to bring you back from the dead? Would one of the dead raise you up? And what happened with that woman earlier? She deserved what was coming; you and I both know that. She violated your law and the world's law. You even confused your own people by saying 'Let he without sin cast the first stone.' Why? You should've picked up a stone and thrown it yourself!"

"Life and death are controlled by *my* hands. Blessed are those who seek my hand, because they carry out the will of God. My ways make life on earth worth living, no matter how long or short it may be," Yahshua responded.

"You know, you should try taking a stand for those that are living righteous for once, instead of people that are the complete opposite. And besides, this world doesn't want to know the truth. They wouldn't know a sin if two or more people committed the same sin, and they wouldn't admit wrongdoing to whoever is on the receiving end of the sin if they were the one committing the sin. Just the other week two men slept with the same prostitute. One slept with her next to the temple and the other..."

"I've had enough of your lies Satan! You have not seen these people. This was a fictional story that was told yesterday. It was a mere moral discussion between two men. The truth is that I have come to earth to bring refuge to the poor man who slept with the prostitute, the man of rank in the Roman and Jewish community that also lay with the prostitute, and also the prostitute involved with both men. Anyone who hasn't *accepted* me will be lost."

Satan was furious yet became fearful of the power of Christ. He was stunned that Yahshua knew what was going on yesterday. I was humbled by what He had said. I had yet to see anyone of power speak with that much passion to stand up for the least of men. I took a moment to join Yahshua in prayer. After which, I received orders to go watch over Kanaar and Jonarbi. Apparently, they were in the same prison.

CHAPTER EIGHT

The three men I saw now were exhausted from being shackled in a standing position. Unfortunately, they did not have the stones to curse God and chew their tongue or bite their wrist. Kanaar was in rough shape yet he did not attempt to escape his agony. The other man I had followed appeared to have a bloody mouth from biting his tongue. He obviously couldn't finish the job. They used their only weapon in their arsenal while being bound in the stench of steel, sweat, and blood. The tainted spirits close by looked entertained by their conversation so far.

"I can't believe this is happening, and so fast. How did I end up in this predicament? I'm not a murderer and I'm sentenced to death. How could this be?" Kanaar asked.

"Relax, perhaps you'll die before they actually start the nailing on Golgotha's hill," said Barabbas.

Jonarbi added, "From what I hear those bastards have no soul or compassion for the condemned. In this sentencing, I hope it's swift. Wishful thinking I guess. I wish I could have a last meal at least."

"Well having a last meal is overrated. My last meal is what got me here in the first place. The surprising thing is Pontius Pilate became more furious than the man I stole the food from. I just knew that I was going to be hanged today. I just knew it. For some reason, this judge lets me live for one more god-forsaken day so the word could travel about my crime. More importantly, everyone will hear about my punishment. These men are going to crucify me tomorrow with a huge crowd to watch."

"You and I both will be the center of attention," Jonarbi said. "You know, now that you mention it, I should've been dead by now too. My trial and sentencing happened right after yours. If I were a betting man, I would say the only reason why I'm still alive is because the sun started to go down. I suppose no one could make a decent spectacle of my shame and execution in the current conditions."

"I wish I were dead or able to kill you wailers, because hearing you talk is depressing."

Jonarbi asked, "Now that we are facing death, do you think we should've taken a chance at Pontius Pilate?"

"This is my only regret," Kanaar answered.

"I did throw a strike at him when I received my sentence. That little jackal ducked when I threw my hook. I ruined my only opportunity. Can you believe that?"

Kanaar asked, "Barabbas, why are you here?"

"I'm here for a whole lot of reasons. I killed people who had it coming. I killed people for being at the wrong place at the wrong time. I killed men for money. I also killed highly ranked people in our society. We've heard your story, Kanaar. Jonarbi, why are you scheduled to die tomorrow? Tell us so I won't kill you too."

"You're a kook, Barabbas, but yes. Tell us what happened. I can't see you clearly but it doesn't seem that you came up around the low-lives like me and Barabbas."

Jonarbi replied, "I'd rather not say. I'm still working on it in my mind. I know that sounds ridiculous but I have to get over it first before I tell my story."

Kanaar asked Jonarbi, "Why aren't you going to tell your story? We've told our story, and you can't tell yours. That isn't fair. Are you afraid we won't understand your great pronunciation of words? Don't be an arrogant bastard about it."

"I just haven't accepted my fate yet; I won't feel comfortable until I can come to terms with it."

Barabbas explained, "I haven't come to terms with it either and I've been here for a while. Unfortunately, you could die before you work it out in your head. Your story is like a coin. That's a pretty big coin to have in your pocket Mr. Robber. None of us are envious of it, because we have our own dirty deeds that have landed us here. At the end of this life, we had our coins and casted our lots in this game of chance. What's the point of having a large and shiny coin if you don't let anyone know that you have it?"

"Well you have a point. I just don't want you or anyone else in my business."

"I don't want your business, trust me. You are the one scheduled to die and you share your fate with Kanaar. Death will greet both of you, but he will pass me by. Please hear my words. I am not envious of your coin. We all have a coin. Are you ashamed of your coin? Do you think your coin shines more than ours, or do you think your coin is dirtier and you simply can't believe that's the one you hold in your pocket?"

Demons were walking around Jonarbi. He said, "I never thought about it like that."

Barabbas replied, "I've been here a while, so allow me to catch you up to speed. I have so many stories that you and Kanaar literally do not have enough time to listen to them all. I have so many coins, and a sadistic grin to go with every one of them. I don't want your coin because I'm so content with my own. I have become rich and wretched with these coins, these stories, these memories, the screams. Yes, the screams. I will be exactly the same with my future intentions, if I'm ever given the chance of freedom. I hold on to them because they are more than a part of me, they are my friends. The weights of them are being held closer than anyone I had on the outside, especially since most of my friends haven't come to visit me yet. However, I am genuinely interested in how you got here. I don't have to touch your coin, but maybe we could see how rough or how smooth the edges are? Can we see how worn the face of this coin looks?"

I thought to myself: I do *not* like Barabbas. Who does he think he is? Is he out of his mind? What I would give for this name to come across my next assignment. This man was twisted and jagged. To makes things worse, Barabbas was crafty with words. I wouldn't trust him with a dead dog. I hope Jonarbi would see that and not take heed in telling Barabbas his life story. I just hope that he was not that low in spirit to be that desperate. There was no good in telling him any information.

"Just think about it. Kanaar and I are not trying to judge here. You made your moves the same way we did. We just want to be your brothers, only if it's just for a while. Take refuge in the fact that we are powerless in these chains. Men in prison only dream of freedom to wake up in shackles. There's no real escape. However, there's no law against freeing your mind."

"He's right. What do you have to lose? Let us live vicariously through you for a while. I'd feel more comfortable knowing the man I'm going to die next to."

"Alright, I'll tell you."

"Well that didn't take too long," I said out loud with disappointment.

"I know this is going to be good."

After a deep breath, Jonarbi began his story by saying, "It all started with how I lived my life, I suppose. I remember it as if it was yesterday, or as a matter of fact, earlier this week. I made the decision that landed me here. I was coming home from a long day's work. When I arrived I was welcomed by my wife and four children. I smiled and they had so much joy just to see me. They all were starting to see me less and less; you know how that goes when it comes to work. I washed my hands and sat down at the dinner table. My wife poured me a glass of my favorite wine. It was dry and full of flavors of different berries."

"We were right. You eat amongst royals don't you?"

"I sipped on the various flavors of wine throughout the daytime. It is my calling and profession. I own four vineyards, or at least I did. I started in the trade under my father, and under him I learned all there is to know. I helped him become successful beyond measure. I saved enough money to finally purchase my own land and started to work on it as time passed. It's the only thing I know how to do, as with my father."

"Well it sounds like you were the "well-to-do" type of man I held my hand out to for spare change."

"I was the man that was able to give. I had done well for myself over time. My wife did her best to help out, and having children always gave me that extra push to go further and to try harder. I wanted to make sure that I could always provide for them. My children could go and play while being in a safe place. I gave them decent clothing that wasn't tattered or ripped at the end, and I made sure they wore sandals that always fit their foot size. That can be a pain. Yet as they grew in size, so did my business. I even had enough money to put into other ventures outside my normal scope of business. At my high point, I owned four vineyards along with two homes that I rented to two other families."

Barabbas asked, "What are you, some sort of super human or immortal? There's only so much time in a day. How did you manage four fields and other properties by yourself?"

"Now don't get me wrong. On my best day, I still wasn't rich. I kept everything local. Everything was within an hour's walking distance from my house. That was for my convenience. However, I do admit that everything was getting strenuous and too big for me to handle completely on my own grit and determination. I had to hire a couple of servants to help me tend to the yards. I rented the homes out to pretty trustworthy people whom I trusted to take care of the property while they occupied the space. I had favor and they did."

Kanaar scoffed, "Yes, you had favor alright. Oh I'm sorry, please continue."

"Back in the early years of working on our own land, my wife and I were able to save enough money to expand. We put our coins together and purchased a second field. We started to have children during that time as well. So we had two vineyard fields and one child. Even though it took much more effort to maintain two fields, we were able to store up money quicker than having simply one field. Those were more humble times, since we could not get any help from anywhere; we had to put our sweat and tears in the field. At that time, every piece of silver we earned came from our daily toil in the field. We had to sell a lot of new wine to cover our expenses. We also had a small line of aged wine that we sold only to select buyers, the more prosperous. Those people could afford that wine and at the price we charged. We were always glad to see those customers come by."

"Sounds like you were gaining momentum in your income stream."

"Indeed. Our income stream thickened. The great thing about having a thicker income is that we did everything in coins. We did not worry about purchasing what we needed or wanted, even though we had our second child a couple years after the second field. If we had the money, we would make a purchase. If we did not have the money, we walked away or did not go to the town square in the first place to protect ourselves from temptation. We saved up a lot of money. The business helped us save so much money that we stopped saving for current liabilities. After we found our stride, we splurged for a while. When my wife and I wanted to do something, or buy something that we honestly could go without, we just did it. We spoiled our children in the way that neither my wife nor I had ever experienced growing up."

"Wouldn't that get attention from the wrong people, you know, people like us?"

"Of course it did. You have to be cautious of the company that you keep. I had good people working with me and good colleagues that had worked for my dad. One became a good friend and the others were good business contacts. I always confided in my wife as well. Over time, people may start to take notice of success and failures, and you meet new people along the way. Some of the people that we met were money lenders."

"I think I know where this is leading," said Barabbas with a sigh.

"They inquired about how our savings had been growing for so long, and also what we did for a living. There's something awkward about how the world operates: when you're not interesting, people avoid you like the plague or simply ignore your existence. When you become a person of interest, you're all of a sudden not hard to find."

Kanaar said, "I don't understand. I would have killed for a money lender to pay any attention to my well-being and personal interest. My money situation was as broke as my arm. Why is this so wrong?"

Jonarbi answered, "You bring up the question that can make a man rich or a slave. None of us are proven fortune tellers in any business. Everything has risks, including the relationships businessmen form. I was initially flattered when the money lenders actually knew me by name and showed interest in my plans. I saw myself as an ordinary head of the household with an average account."

"In laymen's terms can you break down the risks that a businessman faces?" asked Kanaar.

"Sure. Generally, a good relationship with a money lender, or for any business relationship for that matter, is when you make money with a product or service and the lenders make money as well for being your financial partner. A bad relationship with a money lender is when you are not making enough income to cover all of your expenses for the business and your personal livelihood, while still owing money. When you do business with a money lender, they get paid regardless. The risk is that the businessman cannot guarantee that the relationship will be good *after* the loan has been received."

"That makes sense, but it sounds pretty fishy to me. If you're the one running the business, shouldn't it be the other way around?" asked Barabbas.

"I don't get what you are trying to say."

"What I think he is trying to say is, if you're the one doing all the work on the fields, by yourself and occasionally your wife, how come you're not the one being guaranteed money? I'm no professional, but it sounds like the money lenders are guaranteed money if you agree to go into business with them. It sounds like they would tell you how to make the wine if you were to fall on tough times."

Barabbas said with a chuckle, "You should have had us as part of your counsel, for a substantial fee of course."

"That's a little exaggerated, but I get your point. When I entered an agreement with them, I basically started to work hard for their benefit, as if I worked for them."

"I still do not see how this is absolutely terrible. If you worked for yourself or worked for someone else, you're still working. You had a job that you tasked yourself; it's still a source of income. You are still in a much better position than I was. What's the danger in this? I would've traded sandals with you any day of my miserable life. I had real problems."

"So what the hell are you trying to say?"

"Well I think we're both thinking the same thing. You had the wife, the children, the home that you paid for with coins, AND you owned your own business. You just finished telling us that a relationship with money lenders could be good or bad. What happened? You were a thriving businessman. What relationship was so bad with them that you're now facing the death penalty?"

"It sounded good at first, since I never could qualify for someone to take a chance on my business. I figured I would take their money and put it to the same use that I would've done if I were to have coins in-hand, get the same profitable results, and then pay them back the money and interest. I would take a cut, or give the lenders some of what was on top, and keep the remainder. My theory was based on the presumption that even after paying back the money lenders as the weeks and months passed, I would have more in my pockets than simply using my saved coins to fund my operations."

Barabbas asked, "It sounds like the plan made logical sense, but what were you thinking? Why did you fix something that wasn't broken?"

"To be honest, when I remember what I been through with the business and made it out alive, I figured if I had more fields and business relationships to back me up during the good times, they would also be there during the bad. At the time I had three children but the oldest wasn't old enough to work in the field. He needed more time to grow and mature a little. As time passed, I was convinced of what entering an agreement with these people could positively do for my business, so I didn't have too much hesitation on taking out a loan. So I purchased my third field with a loan.

That was my mistake.

"That is shameful. You wouldn't trust your own son to work in your field but you are a businessman just like the money changers and you give them full, unwavering trust just off a small glimpse of the future."

"Yes, and it gets worse. I started to purchase homesteads. I took a few denarii and purchased another house to rent without paying off the field first, which I thought was guaranteed money coming in. After that, I took out a loan to purchase a second house to rent. Both were in great locations near the market centers. They were exceedingly attractive living quarters and I was able to pledge payments towards them with the same great interest rate as my first loan. A year goes by and things are absolutely great. We are making the most money we ever had in our life. Our savings were in great standing, the renters occupying the homes paid in a timely fashion, and we were selling wine out as quickly as we made it. Even King Herod received word-of-mouth about our wine and he became a large purchaser, buying immense quantities of the new and old wine skins. With all of the success we had, we had three loans, two on homesteads and one on a field. During the duration of these loans, we were lucky to have only one slow period with the fields, but the rental income came in steady without fail. I started to feel my success was on my fingertips."

Barabbas asked, "So how did you get the fourth field?"

"I took out another loan."

"Again?" said Kanaar, with a sarcastic, envious tone.

"Yes, and this was my final loan from the money lenders, but it was much different. I had my sights on the outskirts of town. It had lots of grass, trees, and bushes. It looked stable and fertile at a first glance and it grabbed my attention. I told myself that I would be foolish not to take a chance on this piece of land. To me, it looked as precious as gold. The deal wasn't as good as the previous three loans because of the sheer size of the loan and because I had three obligations outstanding. Nevertheless, I talked to them, my wife, and my friends of counsel and they all agreed that it was a great business venture. It was so good that one of my colleagues that no longer was in the wine business co-signed on the loan, just so he could get his fair share of the profits. This helped take some of the debt off of my shoulders too."

"Since you had a co-signer, this must have been a big deal. How much was the agreement that you made with the money lenders and changers?" Barabbas asked.

"Envision this: I had three decent sized fields to work on. I could handle the work on all three fields by myself. This fourth field was at least five times as big as any of three fields that I owned!"

"Wow that is completely deranged. Which side of town was this field located?"

"This was on the west side of town."

"I used to set up camp in those fields from time to time, a truly nice area."

"It sounds like you were trespassing. Since I'm no longer on the other side of this prison cell and can't do anything about it, you get a pass brother Kanaar."

"So this is the part of the story when you hire two workers?" Barabbas asked.

"Yes it is."

"So the money changers trusted you solely with your track record?" Kanaar asked.

"They made the deal based on the condition that I use some of my money to qualify for the loan. I had the money already saved and my fellow colleague offered to put his money down with me, to help provide leverage in the deal."

"Well, at least you weren't alone in the struggle."

"At first everything went exactly as planned. I made more money, yet I had more expenses because of it. I stored up money, but my wife and I splurged even more frequently than before. I know there's a saying, 'don't forget where you came from,' but as more success came in, the less time I reflected on my upbringing. The good times blinded me from my past. This lasted for a few years, until the season drastically changed."

"What do you mean by 'the seasons changed'?"

"Good question. I'm not talking about the seasons like the weather and time of year. I am referring to the cycles of a business. Every vocation has them and so far the family business has survived and thrived through all the slow periods of production. A business can remain flat or stable after rebounding from a recession. After this, a business can grow and thrive as new opportunities come about until it reaches its peak. After the business reaches its peak or the highest level of achievement, the business starts to decline, and may go into a recession period."

Barabbas asked, "So basically the businesses went dry?"

"Yes, all at once."

"That's incredible, in a bad way of course. How did it happen?" Kanaar asked, being intrigued by his hardship.

"First, the rain didn't come down as often as it had in the past. The vineyards need the water for growth and to sustain the plant. Otherwise, the plant will not be as fruitful or it will simply die. There was so much work we had to do maintaining and simply cutting off the dead plants that you wouldn't believe it. Also the weather in general started to go out of normal sequence. Some days would be great, then scorching hot, then abnormally cold for the time of year. The need for wine didn't diminish, but I couldn't produce the quantity necessary to cover our current expenses. I wouldn't decrease our prices of the aged wine so I basically charged a little bit more for the new wine I had. It worked until I ran out of supply of the new wine," said Jonarbi.

"Did you try any vineyard tricks or bring out any new methods?" Barabbas asked.

"I ran through a lot of ideas. With a field of that size, I just knew something would come forth and produce something great. I tried all of the different areas within that given space, and nothing worked. I couldn't turn the corner using that land. I attempted to forfeit the land to satisfy the loan, but they wouldn't allow it. The money changers determined that no one except us was trying to do anything with that land in quite some time. The city was already big enough without expanding residential living spaces so it had no use for the massive area. Since they now heard that I couldn't use it to grow anything, they determined that the land was worth much less than my original loan. Therefore, I still owed money. I owed a lot of money."

"What about your friend and business partner?" Kanaar asked.

"As soon as he found out, he paid me coins to satisfy 'his portion' of the loan. We had a huge argument because he felt that I should be paying more since it was my risk, even though I reminded him that he thought this was a great idea too. The man put in just as much money as I did to sign the loan. So after he gave me his silver, I took it directly to the money lenders. After that, I never saw my partner again. He did not turn out to be a great friend."

"Well, for the record, I hope your old partner gets his in the end. He was so close to you."

"He was a real coward. I'm surprised you didn't kill him for leaving you. I would have, that's all I'm saying. When there's too much money involved, someone is going to get nervous. You should've taken care of the problem the same way I did in my day."

"Who are you telling? You would expect this from a grimy bastard that you don't know. Anyway, even my two smaller fields that I had for so many years were affected by the hard times and they were not producing like they had in the past. I sold those two fields for a profit and took half of the money to pay down the debts. The other half I decided to try my luck at different locations, in search for better days. I couldn't believe the trouble I had. I would try one field and nothing would happen. Then I'd sell that land only to purchase some more land that wouldn't help me produce wine. Eventually, I had to sell the third field because I ran out of ideas. Finally I simply kept the money and that's what my family lived off of."

Kanaar asked, "What about the multiple homes you had?"

"The hard times hit the rentals as well. In the first homestead I purchased, the family suffered a tragic event. The man of the household died. The mother did not work and remained at home to take care of the children. I gave her two months of free living so she could either find work or someone to pay for the rent. Unfortunately, she later had to move out. It took an even longer time to rent the home again. Apparently, people do not want to stay at a house that someone recently passed away in."

"You had some bad luck man, good grief. What about the other home?"

"I had to make a decision. I realized that a business that I grew up learning, practicing, and have mastered now failed me in my time of need. Even though it was still bringing in money I didn't want to risk taking another loss. So I sold the house. Luckily, I sold it at a profit to pay off the loan that it had against it. I simply saved the remainder to pay for things as they came about."

Barabbas asked, "Did you ever get a new resident for your rental?"

"I did eventually but unfortunately it was my only source of income.

All of it went to payment towards the loan. The majority of the family expenses were paid out of our savings. We simply ran out of moves."

"Did your wife truly know how bad everything was? Did your children know?"

"She knew that things weren't as good as it was before, but she didn't know the extent of how bad. Perhaps she didn't want to *accept* the truth of the matter. She simply started to cut back on the nicer things and we both started to be more selective in what things the children picked out and purchased. My wife was really teaching them about the importance of having patience."

"So did you tell her what was really on your mind?" Barabbas asked.

Jonarbi began to stutter and his words became incomplete fragments. He had asked them to give him a moment and the other two men attempted to be empathetic. They couldn't get a fair glimpse of each other at this point. They couldn't see the chains around their wrists but they felt them and knew they were there. Kanaar tried to lighten the mood but it didn't work. Barabbas remained quiet until Jonarbi felt comfortable. In the hallway of the prison, there were a couple of lamps; mainly for the guards to help guide them back and forth through the walkway. Occasionally, a guard would walk by to eavesdrop on the growing conversation. My Lord's commands had not changed.

CHAPTER NINE

Barabbas gave Jonarbi a moment, but his story intrigued him too much. Periodically he would ask Jonarbi the same question. Over and over and over again, the silent man would avoid giving his answer. Jonarbi remained uncomfortable carrying the shame of everything that had happened, and this was a sensitive situation. Even men who do wrong had strong feelings about their wives, I suppose. I was even interested in Jonarbi's answer. It was late at night, and it was officially dark in the prison with an exception of the torch in the walkway. Even their new brother, Kanaar, asked Barabbas to leave the subject alone for a while.

But Barabbas insisted, "Come on, brother. Let this burden go and release it to the wind. Holding on to these things are not good for your mind. This sort of worry could kill you."

"Do you listen to yourself? Does it really matter at this point if he holds on to his feelings or not?" Kanaar wanted to know.

"I've committed my crimes and I'm at peace with it. If we are going down this path that leads to where all bad men go, would you want to go out like some sort of whimpering coward?" Barabbas asked.

"I'm not a coward, you jackal."

"You truly are full of surprises. Those are such big words. Who knew that you would have the stones to come at the notorious killer with such language?"

"I don't want to say it because I'll sound foolish saying it out loud. This honestly isn't a big secret with what happens between a man and his wife during financially stressful situations. You two are men, aren't you? It is pretty obvious why I don't feel comfortable with this fact. Do you really want me to unveil this truth for you?"

After Kanaar and Barabbas answered yes, Jonarbi replied, "The situation at hand did not have any bearing of *change* in the future. This applies to my wife. You know this. My wife has seen the majority of the details of the deals that I have created or agreed to. She knew all the work I had put in to keep everything afloat and knew how hard I worked to find a new way. However, money creates creatures of habits. Even though she knew that the money was running low and she had scaled back on a lot of fancy things, she could not or would not change her initial wants of having new things. It would've been best that she put that energy to think or do new things to create a new income. Every time I brought this idea to her attention, my plea fell on deaf ears. Her focus on material things became a sword that she did not have control over. Therefore, this sword couldn't be put back at her side."

"Could you explain this further, I don't know much about having material things," Kanaar asked.

"Imagine this: how many times can you explain to your wife that *pressure* can originate and multiply by simply mentioning goods or services that are not bare necessities? All along my wife was in the same situation that I was in. Words out of my mouth were not logically received and when I reminded her of what was really going on in our home, she became defensive. For some reason, it had become really hard to complete my sentences. We were in the same boat yet I was started to be looked at as an enemy. She even lashed back from time to time when I had to re-explain everything that was going on. I did have an urge to get angry. That's when I had to start thinking of ways to deal with those thoughts."

"Well, I applaud you for not beating your wife. I've seen a few men come into a prison after other prisoners found out they struck their wives. Those men become very sorry behind bars. I guess you aren't too terrible of a person on the face of things," Barabbas reasoned.

"Thanks. Overall, we did our best not to hide these conversations from our children so they would know some of what was going on, but I was upset during those moments when I had to say something. After those conversations, we would hide our frustrations from the children, yet we would reiterate to them that certain items were off limits. They didn't catch the hint that something was going on, or at least they didn't act like it. They still went to their mother to ask for things behind my back. My wife would reject many requests, but nevertheless she would make those ill-advised purchases just to make them *smile with glee*."

"I've witnessed my mother act the same way," Barabbas said.

Kanaar raised his voice when he said, "Just be honest with us Jonarbi. It sounds like a bad situation when you talk about your wife. I have to ask you something. Did you buy anything for your children that were not a necessity?"

Jonarbi answered, "Yes."

"Be honest here. Have you made any of these purchases for your children, your wife, or yourself while your resources were being drained?" Kanaar asked with curiosity.

Once again, Jonarbi answered, "Yes."

Barabbas couldn't help to say, "It looks like these debts really took a toll on your marriage."

"What is that supposed to mean?"

"I understand that you were upset that your wife spent the hard earned money on herself, her children, and probably on you for material things that didn't matter. You thought that this was not right and somehow you have your right to do the same thing. How are you going to focus your attention on her by pointing the finger? When you point the finger, three fingers are coming back at you. You were doing the same thing she was but it wasn't your fault for your own demise?"

"He has a point there."

"I don't know how to fully explain it. That business was the heartbeat of the family. We lived off of the success of the business. Since I thought of myself as the mastermind behind everything, and I still do, I guess I felt that when I did it, it was much more calculated and the expenses were much more anticipated. When my wife spent our money on foolish things, I felt that she took the money for granted. At the same time, my hands were always conscious. I spent the majority of my time looking out for our best interest."

"Sounds like a double standard to me."

"Trust me. Marriage is a beautiful thing, not only in concept but in real life. But having two people coming together as one is going to have some issues and major twists and turns. The longer you are married to the person, the more you will find out. In some scenarios, you sometimes have to take the fall to keep the unit together. There is nothing equal in a union. We both had double standards that we worked through in order to keep the marriage alive. But what do I know? I'm just a thief dying tomorrow."

"We can't judge. I never found a woman I wanted to marry, or vice-versa. Come to think of it, if an argument got out of hand, I could have lost my temper and killed her."

"It makes sense now that you filled us in. That is the type of pressure men would keep concealed so we won't have to explain this to anyone."

"Thanks Kanaar for hearing me out."

"At least you are admitting the pressures a marriage can endure instead of pretending that everything smells like frankincense. I know I couldn't get married. I robbed a woman and kids for their dinner. If I'd known the man of the household would've been so angry, I would've considered another house to break into."

"All things considered, I did my best to communicate with my wife about the worries I had. She knew the calculated risks we had taken: the positive and unglamorous traits of having vineyards, debt and equity, and taking on more debt. My wife knew the rules of commerce just as well as I did! The plan was great, but playing in this matter of business, there is only one thing that matters—the win. The business doesn't care or have feelings if you lose or you know all of the rules and still lose. Our tens of thousands of coins shrunk to ten thousand. Without slowing down, the ten thousand dwindled to one thousand. Finally our savings showed only a few hundred. Many people can win at this matter of commerce, but we simply lost this go-around."

"Did your wife say anything after you told her what was on your mind?"

"The wife heard what I was saying, yet did not take any heed to it. Instead of repeating myself over and over about the issue, I decided to simply hope for the better and do my best. After that stage and our reserves dropped considerably lower, I simply ignored the current situation."

"So, you just depleted your savings?"

"Yes, indeed. I used a lot of my coins to cover living expenses. On top of that, you can add the splurges we couldn't resist. I also had to pay taxes. Taxes that need to be paid do not disappear because of economic hardship. Caesar still wants his money."

"So when did you decide that you were going to rob somebody?"

"When I started to run low on coins with the money changers, I let my mind run wild. At first, I didn't pay attention to these thoughts because I never stole from anyone before. For some reason, the same idea started to reappear into my head repeatedly. I tried to remain optimistic but eventually crime became a solution to my problem. One night I was sitting and enjoying the company of my wife. The little ones were in another room asleep. I had a cup of my best wine. It was from the small stock that I kept for myself. I had a hard day's work and I attempted to relax. It dawned on me that instead of trying to bring about a new income, I should take the money from those who already have an income."

"Have you considered asking for help from other loved ones and friends?"

"I was too proud to beg for money, no offense. I didn't want to be seen in this condition. Also, the charities and communities would look at me as being absurd and be skeptical of providing me funds to support my family in the first place. Even if someone were to take pity and give us a helping hand, if I were to humbly return to them a second month they would turn me down. People will probably think that I had thirty days to turn my entire world right-side up again and would've raised eyebrows upon my arrival. Family, friends, and institutions alike would simply think that I took my turn and their good deed was already finished."

"That is kind of harsh. Are you saying all people would give if it only required a short-term commitment?" Barabbas asked.

"No. All people are not bad, but the societies we live in are terrible. I was one of the bigger money movers outside this room of chains, cold air, and despair. *I am one of them.* Who else would know how a man or woman would be treated if they were to fall on tough times? I gave to charities and people in need before, but honestly I had never prayed, and I really don't know what prayer is. I never truly hoped for anyone I've helped to come back to me if things haven't turned a corner in their favor. I wanted all of the misfortunate to go away so I wouldn't have to give in the first place. This is definitely how I felt, even in the initial process of doing a good thing. Somehow I thought that if I gave a couple coins, there would be this mystical chain reaction of great things that will happen for this person and he or she would never have to ask me about anything ever again. I considered my generosity as a one-and-done situation. I gave so I could walk away with a grin of satisfaction. Even in the back of my mind I hoped that if things were to get more prosperous for myself, I would be further and further removed from these people."

"You sound like you are cold and heartless, but you also sound like everyone else I ever came into contact with."

"Am I speaking lunacy? Have you ever seen any organization run by the people that are in need? It would make sense to give them a chance to be in charge of some little things so they can provide for themselves, and the end result would be many less people who would be ultimately in lack. But no, this will never be the case."

After a demon entered Jonarbi's mouth, he added, "So after looking at my situation and coming to terms of where I stood, the only rational thing for me to do was to do something *selfish*. I came to the conclusion that robbing someone and my initial thoughts of doing well for humanity were so similar that it was hard to judge which position was more selfish at the end of the day. I *gave* all in the name of *taking* more for myself. This world we live in doesn't truly care about our personal circumstances. No one treats each other as we would treat ourselves. Before putting ourselves in another person's sandals, we will judge the maker and craftsmanship of them. I saw myself filled with *darkness*. In this prison cell I am still drenched with so much darkness that I do not recognize myself. On the outside, it didn't matter if I walked in an open field or in a lavishly decorated room; I always felt the place where two walls meet."

"Couldn't you reach out to one of your well-to-do friends or associates about how to deal with these types of problems? Wasn't there anybody you could talk to?"

"I didn't want to come off as a burden to anybody. What could they do? Take me to the temple? Or maybe some sort of deity? Someone had already extended their hand in fellowship and believe it or not, I actually went. Nobody cared to show me any of this during the rise of my success. Why should anyone care about me now that everything turned sour?"

"Well, you could've tried. You didn't have anything to lose, Jonarbi."

"Kanaar you are right. However, we both know how it feels when we've tried to do right, yet our efforts were in vain. I bet you'd also say there are many men who have a heavy load on their shoulder, you know, that memory or desire that would give them all the motivation and drive they would need to take action. Well I am truly blessed because I was balanced. I carried my hardships on both of my shoulders. On one, I had the pressure to provide, even though there was nothing in sight in which I could work with. The other burden is the lives that were sustained solely by my performance. With my thoughts in my head, I had my wine and grinned. My eyes were set on the prize that I had to win. If I robbed, all of that could be a memory. I could be free. Then I could start over. I had made up my mind. If it's a man's pocket, I would reach for them. If it's a woman's pocket, I would extend my hand and fist. Nothing mattered anymore. I no longer called these worries an enemy but my ally."

"You sound just as lonely I am," said Kanaar.

"A single thought came to me while drinking my fine wine that evening. I hoped if I was truly as dark as I felt, then nobody could see me at night."

"Unfortunately, you were not dark enough."

CHAPTER TEN

The voice of the Lord led me to leave the prison and go back to the garden of Gethsemane. When I arrived, Yahshua was praying in the middle of the garden. Although Satan was there as well, He raised his eyes towards the stars. Yahshua was no longer concerned about the presence of His enemy, or the blood that trickled down from his head.

As I sat down near Yahshua to write in the holy scroll, He began his prayer:

Father, the hour has come. Glorify Your Son, that Your Son also may glorify You, as You have given Him authority over all flesh, that He should give eternal life to as many as You have given Him. And this is eternal life, that they may know You, the only true God, and Jesus Christ whom You have sent. I have glorified You on the earth. I have finished the work which You have given Me to do. And now, O Father, glorify Me together with Yourself, with the glory which I had with You before the world was.

I have manifested Your name to the men whom You have given Me out of the world. They were Yours, You gave them to Me, and they have kept Your word. Now they have known that all things which You have given Me are from You. For I have given to them the words which You have given Me; and they have received them, and have known surely that I came forth from You; and they have believed that You sent Me. I pray for them. I do not pray for the world but for those whom You have given Me, for they are Yours. And all Mine are Yours, and Yours are Mine, and I am glorified in them. Now I am no longer in the world, but these are in the world, and I come to You. Holy Father, keep through Your name those whom You have given Me, that they may be one as We are. While I was with them in the world, I kept them in Your name. Those whom You gave Me I have kept; and none of them is lost except the son of perdition, that the Scripture might be fulfilled.

But now I come to You, and these things I speak in the world, that they may have My joy fulfilled in themselves. I have given them Your word; and the world has hated them because they are not of the world, just as I am not of the world. I do not pray that You should take them out of the world, but that You should keep them from the evil one. 16 They are not of the world, just as I am not of the world. Sanctify them by Your truth. Your word is truth. As You sent Me into the world, I also have sent them into the world. And for their sakes I sanctify Myself, that they also may be sanctified by the truth. I do not pray for these alone, but also for those who will believe in Me through their word; that they all may be one, as You, Father, are in Me, and I in You; that they also may be one in Us, that the world may believe that You sent Me. And the glory which You gave Me I have given them, that they may be one just as We are one: I in them, and You in Me; that they may be made perfect in one, and that the world may know that You have sent Me, and have loved them as You have loved Me.

Father, I desire that they also whom You gave Me may be with Me where I am, that they may behold My glory which You have given Me; for You loved Me before the foundation of the world. O righteous Father! The world has not known You, but I have known You; and these have known that You sent Me. And I have declared to them Your name, and will declare it, that the love with which You loved Me may be in them, and I in them.[1]

My heart was filled with joy once I heard this. Lucifer trembled when the words reached his ears. The serpent didn't know exactly how to respond. He felt He was really the chosen one from the Most High, yet Yahshua was his opposition. I wanted to interfere and remove Satan from the garden, yet I stood by and watched vigilantly. I remembered the two men that I saw in the prison with Barabbas. Since Yahshua prayed for all men and women without limitation, maybe there was hope for them after all. I think Yahshua would have his work cut out for Him with those two—but nothing is impossible. Meanwhile, Satan was greatly perturbed because he was stunned and in awe of Christ's words. However, he would never admit that.

"I'm sorry that you are going to fail your God in heaven. This will never be done, never. You're no different than regular men because you make promises to the real God that you can't keep. You are not residing in glory, your highness. You're down here, in the flesh, like everyone else. That God won't save you from any pain," Satan said. "You seem to be a little slow so I will help you out here. Go home and sleep eternally so you will not bear this pain and punishment. You'll be dead and you won't come back to life. At least you won't have any shame to bear. No one will have to know about it. If you refuse, I will ensure that the blood will flow from your body until death. This is your choice."

Yahshua said nothing to him. He boldly stood up and headed towards His disciples to check on them. Since the devil was not a fan of people being gathered together that love Yahshua, he followed at a distance. He hoped that Yahshua would want to pray by himself some more. When Yahshua reached His men, He was disappointed yet calm. The men that were supposed to be keeping watch for any danger were asleep. They were also supposed to join Yahshua in prayer. After waking them and having a quick word, He headed back into the garden to pray.

"Doesn't that upset you, even just a little bit? Those men are supposed to be your friends; you washed their feet and broke bread with them. Now, these men can't even follow simple orders? Why can't they even do what is natural as a human being? They are acting like they never were your friends. They didn't support you then and won't care in the future. What's the point of making such a sacrifice? Don't you see the vanity in all of this?"

After Yahshua prayed, He rose to his feet and went to find His disciples. Unfortunately, He saw them with their eyes shut. He woke them up and pleaded that they stay awake and watch guard. Yahshua returned to the garden to await his old foe.

"Why have you not returned home yet? Enough is enough. You say you are the Christ, yet your disciples don't obey your commands. Where is your power? I don't think you are as strong and mighty as the people say."

Yahshua replied, "I am as strong as my Father makes me. You are not as strong and mighty as the people say."

Satan shook his head. "It would be a shame that you go through all of this and the people still will not accept that you are whom you claim to be, a savior. You are a legend, a mere myth. You don't scare me, and I know who you are. You should leave their fate to me, and I'll give you rest. I'll make sure that their journey leads to the gates of eternal flames. Their walk will be gradual, some changes of scenery from time to time to keep their damnation interesting and tasteful, but nothing so out of the normal like 'salvation' to disrupt their good time. These people will enjoy all the earthly pleasures along the way. You know, the things they know aren't righteous but they desire it. I'll be their god and my regime will provide ample opportunity for them to spit in your face and on your law. You hate my words but that's what they will do. They are no stronger than you in the flesh. You won't follow God till the end. The burden is so big, yet my hands have calluses to handle this issue. I'll carry this burden; you will live your life, and go about your business elsewhere—like first telling your little friend with his scroll to mind his own business."

I yelled, "That's enough you wicked, ungrateful, twisted..."

Yahshua looked in my direction and His eyes commanded respect and attention, like a father looking intently at his child when they are getting out of hand. He didn't say anything verbally to me but wanted me to watch and pray. So I did. The emotion on His face said everything. Yahshua did not hold my outburst against me. For a third time, He stood to his feet and went to his disciples. Unfortunately, Yahshua saw the same outcome upon His arrival. He spoke to the men once more, and then returned to the garden.

"This is almost too painful to watch. You know, that man that you called out at supper is on his way, but I guess you already knew that since you are the Christ. You may be a scrawny man but you have able limbs. Why don't you run away from here?" Satan asked. "Your disciples won't hold it against you. Nobody will think you are just another Jewish coward. It could be our little secret."

CHAPTER ELEVEN

"I can't stand Him damn it," Satan always said to himself. "His influence is so strong that men (and women) who have never seen Him before may form an opinion of Him, and He won't ever leave them no matter what their track record. Yahshua might have the power to claim hundreds, thousands, or even more back into God's plans but He has unearthly people skills. I don't like His sandals, or His robe, and I *HATE* his parents. If King Herod had ever come within a stone's throw of Joseph and Mary, I wouldn't have this headache in the first place."

The adversary had spoken with the one who ranks as Most High every day since Yahshua was born, begging for the day to test Him. Satan wanted to test Yahshua in a way that would push Him to His death, yet he was not granted the opportunity. He had not received permission to create an even greater mess of things. He looked foolish, yelling from outside the golden gates. The results of those meetings never came out in his favor. But he always decided to push on and find out how far God would go for his beloved human creations. The smallest thing could discredit everything that Christ had ever done. If two or more witnessed Yahshua as a hypocrite, a gossiper, or displaying no compassion towards another person, His entire ministry would come to a glorious end and result in victory for the evil one. Creating chaos was the beast's objective and his plea, but God chose not to answer him yet. He was a long way from heaven, and truly jealous that more and more people were passing away, but they honored God's law and took a strong liking to Yahshua.

While being in the midst of Yahshua and the evil one, I began to pray. I closed my eyes to remember what happened earlier this evening. Before I joined the Lord and His twelve disciples as the Father commanded me, I was given the task to bring some men and women to the foot of His throne. It was then that I set my sights across the land to find the chosen few. After the deeds were finished, I ascended to heaven to bring God's acquaintances, friends, and total strangers to His throne while his darkness lurked from behind. I really thought he was out of his mind. The world would be a better place without him. The men and women were so misled and demented that I'm not confident it would matter if Satan left earth. People did not love one another.

I yelled, "Stay out of my way you fool! Stay away! Keep behind me!"

He fell back and trailed me from a distance. He continued to follow with his terrible comrades. I wondered if my wish would come true and he would destroy himself. I wished only the worst for the serpent, yet my hope was only with God's glory and His commands. The world viewed my hands as unwanted trouble; my heart was with God — always.

I finally reached the heavenly gates. I knelt before the Lord, and I had great joy that many of His own had come home. It was amazing when God leaned forward and called them by name. It was a holy moment when God reached down towards the men or women one by one. He was glorified by their utterances and humbleness. For many of them it was not the first time that they fell to their knees, cried out to the Lord, and simply gave Him praise. God's hand would touch them, and wipe their tears from their eyes. So much pain that these people had endured throughout the years, trusting and believing the faith that was passed down from generation to generation. Finally, the reunion came, and God opened the gates for them.

Soon after the men and women entered God's gracious abode, I arrived and walked boldly towards the entrance. The large gate suddenly slammed behind me with a loud clang. All of the angels that stood near had an aggressive look towards the common enemy. My brothers were not concerned with anyone causing harm in the presence of the Lord, but they had grown accustomed to Satan being an outcast. My brethren stood on guard. As the noise rang throughout the heavens, my hands gripped the old steel. In a reflex, I drew my blade and commanded that he leave at once. Although I was inside the gates, I flew towards the demon while staring the corrupted creatures in their eyes.

God told me, "You have nothing to fear."

My feet touched the streets of gold once again and I returned my sword to its resting place. I watched the snake's remarks. Satan approached God with caution, for he knew that He was all-knowing and all-powerful. God felt his intentions and knew his heart begged for blood. God saw all his efforts before Satan made them. Satan came with a plan of attack. Nevertheless, God allowed his presence for a moment.

"I'm glad to receive greetings and warmth here. It never gets old," the evil one stated.

"How does the warmth you received compare to hell?" I asked.

"I come with my fellow brothers in peace. You draw your weapon from inside the gates, while we reach for nothing?"

"So you want to be civil?"

"Of course, and what exactly was your intention approaching me with one sword against thirty of my strongest earth dwellers?"

"This blade can skewer you and six of them with one strike. I'll take those odds any day. What do you want?"

"It's the same thing I've wanted for a few decades now. Once I receive consent from your chief commander, it is curtains for all of you. Why don't you make your next move your best move? Come join me and be on the winning side."

"Excuse me?"

"The dark shadows and I have conjured up a plan. The truth is, you will be a great asset to us. With your spiritual gift backing our cause, we will be unstoppable."

"My gift comes from my heavenly Father. Even after years of working and toiling with my appointment, I would only do so under His direction. No thanks."

Hell's leader turned to his constituents for some assistance. He raised his hand, and immediately received a reaction from those that stood around him. Some of them reached into their cloak and pulled out a small bag with a tie at the opening. Four of these items were retrieved and tossed towards the devil in charge. After catching them, he turned back towards me juggling the sacks.

"Don't you see how freely my soldiers give? It is only because they know that there is more where that came from," the devil said.

I responded, "I do not follow. Are you attempting to bribe me you old fool?"

"Absolutely not, but I am interested in giving you an opportunity. Surely you stand on streets paved with gold, but all of that is owned by your heavenly Father. He is only allowing you to be there because of His grace. You don't want to be a silver spoon-fed chump your entire existence. Trust and believe me, I know that feeling. Don't you want to earn your money and have power over something? Do you have any pride?"

"You are as pathetic as when I last saw you. I'll pass."

He tried to entice me by showing the contents of what was inside the bags. Being patient with his offer, I saw his hands slowly pour from the bag gold, diamonds, and rubies presented in that order. However, I knew those jewels would cause me to forfeit my place in God's kingdom. Meanwhile, there was still peace amongst the rest of my brothers. They turned their attention to God as Satan wasted air. God's infinite wisdom knew that Satan would never shut up. My short temper wanted to shut him up. Unfortunately, that tempter would win the battle every now and then against weaker prey. Sometimes, a man's soul would be doomed because of a failed test. Even after all of God's wonders, His own believers and followers could become weakened and weary.

Satan began to repeat his claim that Yahshua was not God's true and faithful servant. He told Him that even the Son of Man can become crippled in human flesh. He told God that His spirit is willing but His flesh would become weak and will be destroyed. He exclaimed that if He would give him the chance, he would prove once and for all who the King of Kings is — a weak bastard. He described the worst beating of all time to God and that it would be too much for anyone to bear. Satan elaborated how the pain and the shame would overwhelm Yahshua, and men would be blinded from His truth forever. I witnessed it all, and wanted to bring forth silence. I became restless.

Surprisingly, God finally answered him saying, "Yahshua will be the perfect example of how to live a life the way I intended it to be. He will do many marvelous things for the people whom I love. In all things my son will be strong. The members of my kingdom have been tested in many ways, but never in this fashion. However, He will complete His task with no fear. My son will not fail. Only you are able to come within arm's reach of him. Only you will fail."

Satan trembled, yet he was rejuvenated when God released him to move forward in wreaking havoc once again. This time, it was all or nothing.

Satan had a hard task ahead of him, but even then I began to feel his spirit raise high in excitement. He had a grin that would scare himself if he'd caught a glimpse of his reflection. How did a spirit have so many rows of teeth? On top of this, the legion of high-ranked demons also became infected by his sadistic ways.

"You should have taken my offer, but it's over. I'm going to expose Christ for who He truly is, and everyone alive will witness His shame." Then he turned to me, "Since you refused my gracious hand of wealth and self-purpose, I will find one who will make an agreement for silver!" the serpent boasted.

God instructed them all to leave his presence, so they did so at once. They journeyed back to earth. I stayed at the Most High's feet until peace was restored, remaining until I received His encouraging word. I prayed. That was when a good friend tapped me on the shoulder.

"Do not worry, old friend," Gabriel said.

"I won't. All I do know is that he is never up to any good. What will he do now?" I asked.

"Do not pay any attention to his intentions. You have your orders. Remember to write in your holy scroll. Maybe it will take your mind off of things."

"Do I really need to do more work at a time like this? Don't you see what is happening?"

"Who couldn't see what took place a minute ago? I am in shock with everything to be honest, but trust me on this one. Continue your work. Everything else is details. Besides, all of our assignments are a little different than usual this time around."

"I will trust in the Father. I must return to earth now."

As I opened my eyes, I was alarmed by the sounds of thunder from the ground. Footsteps and the clinging sounds of military fashioned uniforms filled the air. I put away my scroll and drew my sword. I wasn't angry because of the many demons that trampled the ground with the soldiers, but I was vexed about the misguided and confused man that led them here. How dare Judas betray Yahshua and our Father by leading them here? There is no room for a lukewarm body in my Father's kingdom, and I hated the mere sight of Judas Iscariot. Yet I could only stand there on guard, waiting for commands to seal his doom. So I stood there waiting to hear the words and when the soldiers appeared, the words were never spoken. Upon their arrival, and seeing Judas was in front, Yahshua rose to His feet and stood still.

When one of the soldiers asked Him if He was the man named Yahshua, He answered, "I am He."[2]

CHAPTER TWELVE

Yahshua was arrested. I couldn't believe Judas turned on his friend. The officials put the shackles on Him like He was the worst man alive and whipped Him with the same chains. The officials threw punches and spat on Him. My Father gave me specific instructions to only follow Christ, so I did. I followed the group into the Sanhedrin, where they accused Him of all sorts of contradicting charges. They misconstrued His miracles to be some sort of dark magic, or devil worship — anything but acts of God. They chanted His sentence of death over and over and the noise sent rumbling vibrations in the ground. For whatever reason, a cock crowed somewhat near the crowd and Peter grew upset. The angry mob of so-called high priests grew violent. They unanimously decided to put Yahshua in prison and out of their sight. The priests and the surrounding men started to plot what to say to Pontius Pilate as they took Him. They dragged Yahshua out of their court and towards the prison. Three angels joined me as I watched.

He stumbled into the main room. A guard punched the Messiah in the ribs as He walked. He was not a weak man, but the guard who threw the blow wasn't small in stature. My Lord took more punches as one of the soldiers left to find the guard who had the keys to the cell. The devil didn't waste any time and made the most of that moment, stirring more hate all around Christ. Yahshua couldn't gain solid footing. The men hit Him repeatedly and His adversaries made it a sport.

The soldier returned with unfortunate news. He could not find the key to the cells that were separate from other criminals. However, the guard did have the keys to the cells for condemned criminals that awaited their execution or extended prison sentences. The idea appealed to them, for they thought Christ was a troublemaker. The soldier pointed the group in the direction that they must go.

Yahshua braced himself for what would happen. He looked up and quickly asked for God's strength. A soldier lunged into Him with his shoulder. His body flew down the stairs without much control. The chains hit His body hard as Yahshua hit the landing. With a huge laugh, the soldiers lifted Him up by the shackles that had bound Him. I was disgusted at this sight. Furthermore, the soldiers pushed Him down the next set of stairs.

Jonarbi, Kanaar, and Barabbas heard the loud thump and clash of steel. That interrupted their conversation and brought their attention to see what caused this sudden noise. This time the soldiers waited for Yahshua to get Himself back on His feet. The men continued to push and spit on Him as they lead Him to the cell. The chains grew louder and louder as the group came closer to the three cellmates. It was dark, so the men led with a lit torch. The prisoners heard some of the guards' insults and the groans of a man who has been through a lot.

"Whoa, do you hear that?" Kanaar asked.

"Yes, it sounds like someone is feeling the pain. You know it's discouraging when a man is led down this hallway, but that's the worst I've ever heard," Barabbas said.

"He sounds like he's in worse shape than us, Jonarbi. Did you hear the men spit on him?"

"Yes I heard. The shackles do not lie. Those men want to harm him."

The soldiers decided to put Yahshua in the cell across from the other three prisoners. The torch temporarily shined light on them. Yahshua had fresh wounds on his face and He couldn't stand straight because of a bruised rib cage. Yahshua looked briefly in the cells across the way and He saw the men. The criminals caught His gaze. Once the prison cell door was opened, Yahshua was shoved inside. The guards chained Him to the wall in a standing position because that was protocol for the worst criminals. After taking their last strikes at Him, they slammed the steel door closed with a loud clang. One guard locked the cell, and the men walked away to leave them in the darkness.

Curiosity bubbled inside of Barabbas so he asked Him, "Who are you? What is your name? Can't you talk?"

"Maybe he just wants to be alone with his thoughts. I cannot blame him," Jonarbi stated.

From a couple of cells down the hallway, an accomplice and fellow comrade of Barabbas spoke, "I saw his face before Barabbas. This isn't some ordinary man here; at least He is not believed to be like us entirely."

"So who is he?"

"Well that man is rumored to be the king of all the Jews. His name is Yahshua. He is supposed to be all powerful or something," the man answered.

Barabbas replied, "Is that right? So you are the big man in charge of everything, including this prison? I never saw the warden down this hall before."

All of the prisoners got a laugh out of it. There were a total of fifteen prisoners there, and two of them were scheduled to die tomorrow. No one was certain about what was in store for Yahshua tomorrow, but it didn't look good. I saw all the prisoners and their interests shift towards Yahshua's direction. Although it is dark, I am able to see the heat from all of the men's bodies throughout the hallway. An advantage of being a heavenly being I suppose. The other three angels were still with me. Unfortunately, our enemy was here as well.

"Tell me. What did you do to end up here? Did you embezzle the Jew's money and make some bad deals?"

"Barabbas is giving you a hard time. I'm going to step aside and let him handle my concerns. I want to see how this comes to pass," Satan added.

"I will give a wager that he used some mystical powers like the hand readers have done. He probably removed one desperate soul's heart of hopelessness and gave him some vision to aspire to before they died," Kanaar added.

Yahshua responded, "The hand of the righteous will die while feeling compassion for another person, and giving what he has freely to someone else."

Kanaar was stunned at the response he received, and could not think of a jeer that could negate anything that Yahshua had said. I knew it struck a nerve because his posture changed. Even though my Master was beaten, weak, and now exhausted from standing a long period of time, it did not bother Him. Satan didn't like that at all. He yelled for the other demons to join him.

"So are you just another one of those prophets who teaches some sort of divine wisdom? Don't you think that your image is a little tarnished, being behind bars?" Jonarbi asked.

"What do you have to say to that?" Satan uttered.

A fellow demon added, "I think Jonarbi is going to burst. His misfortune has blinded him like the other cellmate. He is definitely a lost cause."

"I do not care for your cavalier spirit acting holier-than-thou inside of a prison," Jonarbi went on to say. "We are going to die tomorrow, and they might kill you too since two men are already officially scheduled. If you are a king from above, how come your angels or your followers aren't here to fight the guards in your defense? How come your holiness isn't bright enough to bring any light into this dark hallway?"

Yahshua remained silent. The evildoers wore smirks on their faces. Even Barabbas was amused and all the more curious as to how Yahshua would react in the hopeless situation. In my eyes, they were all hopeless, and simply lived to bring another person down to their level of hopelessness. One of the demons felt rejuvenated and had a spark in his eye after witnessing this. He attempted to take a lunge at Yahshua. He quickly took a few steps from the criminal's cell through the steel door, headed towards Yahshua at a blistering speed. One of the angels saw him and tackled the creature, forcing him a few paces away from the target. The other demons were upset, so I drew my sword.

"You are going to pay for that," I said.

The dark shadow responded, "Your beloved savior will pay first! You don't have a chance against us. All of the scriptures are beautiful songs until every situation turns against your obedience to them. Yahshua is all talk and can't take the burden of sin from everyone."

I walked closer to the cursed vermin and raised my blade over my head. I had heard enough. I narrowed my eyes onto my target, but another angel urged me to stop, reminding me that it was not the time. I resigned my campaign yet I was too irritated to enter the cell with Yahshua. I remained in the hallway, to monitor the prisoner's movements closely. Suddenly, Yahshua decided to break His silence again.

"I will trust in you, Father. With everything that I have, I will trust you. My Father, give me strength. I will give myself away as a sacrifice, even though a man robs us," Yahshua prayed.

"What do you mean a man robs us?" Barabbas asked.

Kanaar raised his voice and asked, "Did someone in here rob Yahshua?"

No one said that they did. Many of them had heard of Yahshua before, yet there wasn't a man in the prison that had met Christ directly. Barabbas had not robbed Him nor did Kanaar. That is when the attention turned to Jonarbi.

"Jonarbi, who did you steal from? Did you take from this man's pockets?" Barabbas asked.

"No," he responded.

"Did you take from His relative perhaps?"

"I didn't think I did initially."

"Well, you either did or you didn't. Who did you plot against?"

"I know I messed up bad, but not this bad. I ended up robbing a temple. Actually, I robbed two temples. I was caught when I robbed the bigger one. Apparently, since they serve the same god, the word spread; so the bigger temple was alerted. The high priests witnessed me breaking in and taking money."

Kanaar added, "You are finished. I thought I was going to hell."

"I am not a Jew. I didn't know that when I robbed a temple that I would meet the prophet who was over all of it. Even so, I don't know Him, and He won't show me any mercy. His followers sure didn't. Do you want to know what I discovered? The same people who gave offerings to a god they've never seen are the same people who don't care about anyone outside those four walls. What is all of the obedience and their abundance worth if they couldn't share the wealth cheerfully?"

"Well that's all a heap of dung. I don't think the real god or the child of the real god would be in a jail with us, "Kanaar said.

I was surprised that Jonarbi actually admitted who he stole from, never mind told Barabbas. It looked like this man was in need of some better company. Although Yahshua was right across from those three criminals, they did not recognize that they stood in the presence of their saving grace. There was no faith in those cells. It was all gloom even though Yahshua had started to address them both. Nevertheless, Yahshua revealed His power. He didn't change His spirit and outlook in order to fit in. Meanwhile, the men continued to talk amongst themselves.

"My stomach is grumbling, but I don't want to eat again. I don't see the point," Kanaar complained.

"All of this erratic talk about me stealing money from some god has created an appetite. We should yell for a guard to give us some bread," Jonarbi responded.

"I don't know about that. They already fed us once today because they had to. I'm not asking. It's bad enough that we are dying tomorrow," Kanaar groaned. "I don't want any additional beatings than what is already coming."

"We are grown men. Surely one meal can sustain life but I want more."

"That guard will rub the food in the ground and force you to eat it for sport. They probably spat in our food earlier."

"Now you are just being paranoid," Jonarbi said.

"Kanaar has a point. Besides, there is another reason why you should tell yourself that you are not hungry or thirsty," Barabbas interjected.

"What are you talking about?"

"It's simple. What do you smell?"

"Dung."

"This is my point. There's only one way it gets to smell this bad in here. To add insult to injury, your hands are chained at your head's height. It seems like you would've figured this out by now."

"Excuse me for not knowing. I'm only going to be here one night, unfortunately. Barabbas, do you think we are going to get some clean clothes tomorrow?"

"Yes, probably. And after the whipping and beatings, your clothes may be pretty torn up. They are going to try to take your life during the scourging. I heard a story of a man losing his bowels while being beat."

"Is that true?"

"Or was it while the man hanged on the cross when he soiled himself? I don't remember what that Roman guard told me. I was just relieved that I wasn't going to experience it."

Yahshua continued to pray silently. I looked towards the heavens and orders had not changed, which meant I would stay here. God must have another angel to take care of tonight's transitions. Satan did not want the criminals to overhear Yahshua. He did not want the condemned to have any hope. I witnessed the devil call out to his fellow brethren from under. As a result, the criminals' fear would ultimately lead to mindless chatter, conversations that lead to nothing, people running in circles, and babbling.

"I don't have any close family or friends that are going to see me soil myself tomorrow, thank goodness. Even if I did, it would not change my future so who cares."

"It is easy for you to say that Kanaar. I have a family," Jonarbi said.

Kanaar asked, "Do you want your wife and children to witness all of this tomorrow?"

"I don't know. I don't want it to be a mystery about what happened to me, but I don't want them to see me treated with less regard than a stray dog."

"That would be disheartening."

"I don't want to lose my dignity in front of them."

"Let's say that doesn't happen, then would you want them there?" Barabbas asked.

"I don't know. I know that my wife will be there once she hears of what happened. We entered our marriage with one understanding. We are together until death."

"That's a nice gesture. I just wonder what will happen afterwards. I've seen so many different gods. When I die, is there any hope for men like us?" Kanaar asked.

Jonarbi answered, "I don't know. It doesn't look like it. What could be done that could save a couple of bandits from the eternity they deserve? Do you think there is a heaven or a better place to go?"

"I want to say yes. There has to be something better out there. You know I don't know anything religious and never had any money for an offering, but there's probably hundreds if not thousands of heavens. I just hope that I see one of them from the inside," Kanaar answered.

"It sounds too good to be true, but it sounds better than what I got. Who decides who gets into your heaven, Kanaar?"

"I think there are three kings that would decide our fate: Minos, Aeacus, and Rhadamanthus. That is, if we get across the river Styx."

"What is Styx, Kanaar?" Jonarbi asked with curiosity.

"I've heard it is the river that stands between life and death. Yet, there is one problem. There is a ferryman, Charon, who will only take us across the river if we have money to pay him. We have to be buried properly with gold placed under our tongue."

After thinking about what he said, Jonarbi replied, "We have two problems. The first problem is that we don't have any gold quinarii or gold aureus in our possession. Also, do you think these Roman officials would give us a proper burial? They have already beaten us half to death. If my wife were to claim my body, do you think the officials would take me down so she could bury me properly and I could have a chance of entering heaven?"

Barabbas interjected, "The Roman guards had taken their beliefs into the very prisons as well. Even if I took pity on both of your current situations and wanted to give you a coin to die with, the chains prevent me from giving you anything. I'm sorry about this, but it looks like we are all headed to Hades, or some place."

"Where could someone go other than heaven or Hades?" Jonarbi asked. "I thought those were the only two places in the afterlife."

Kanaar answered, "Unfortunately, we won't be able to reach the judges on our own accord. Since we do not have money to pay Charon, he will not allow us to come on board. We will remain by the riverside for all eternity. Even if we were good people and were heading to one of the heavens after we were judged, it will not happen unless we had money to pay the ferryman to get to the other side of the river."

"Kanaar, our future appears to be dim indeed. We will be surrounded by emptiness forever according to this belief. If none of the story is true, we are damned to hell because of our crime."

"Who knows, maybe the judges in the afterlife will have some sympathy. Maybe before a final decision is made, we can get a second try at a life on earth. Maybe we can come back as a different person somehow, and live again to prove ourselves worthy. That way when that life ends, we would be buried properly with money to pay Charon."

"I like your thinking Kanaar."

Kanaar added, "Then we could get into those pearly gates with ease. I hope I get a second chance or a chance to be born again to re-enter this world. Start over fresh."

"As a matter of fact, I'm going to ask Minos, Aeacus, and Rhadamanthus to spare me and to think of granting me a second chance right now," Jonarbi said with high expectations.

"I'm right with you."

I couldn't believe what I saw. These men truly would not believe a man sent from the true and living God existed. They also had enough arrogance to look down on Yahshua simply because He was in prison. Kanaar still thought his own mind and brain power was more reasonable than asking Yahshua more questions about life. The other man robbed a temple where Yahshua may have worshipped and taught and he had yet to apologize for what he had done. I didn't understand why those two should be allowed to live. I couldn't take the blasphemous comments any longer. I had the urge to take their lives to show them the real God, just to prove a point. However, the three angels encouraged me to continue to observe their actions. I had seen enough for one night but I had to follow through. I was grateful that all of the men finally passed out from exhaustion, except Yahshua.

CHAPTER THIRTEEN

I looked up above and prayed from time to time. I needed to know what my Father wanted. However, the message had not changed so I stayed here a little longer. Early Friday morning Yahshua began to pray. He had a look of determination. He prayed continuously while the sun started to rise. Christ spent the majority of the time praying for others. He pleaded to His heavenly Father that they will be forgiven, not only by Him but also by the men or women that were offended with the sin. The evil one spoke to Yahshua.

"I give it to you. You are one tough man, aren't you? You still think you can pull this off?" the prince of darkness asked.

Yahshua answered, "Forgiveness takes energy. God does not give up on His people so easily."

"It seems that if you were all powerful and sent from the All Mighty you would have a little bit more flair. You look like the average man before being sent to the gallows."

"I have already conquered the world; you lost."

"We will see it about that. All of us, except..."

"I already know what you are going to say. That will not deter me."

"Why are you so zealous? Doesn't the Son of Man feel any

compassion?"

"More than you'll ever know. I know that my friend Judas has fallen, yet it does not change anything. It is irrelevant to God's will for me."

"Your friend has gone against you. He betrayed you. Doesn't it make you angry? He died the coward's way and took his own life. Judas hanged himself. Knowing all of your ways did not save his life. When the people hear what he has done they will discard all of the wonderful things that he had spoken in your name and all of the miracles he had performed for the lost sheep of Israel. Most importantly, your law and precepts won't save your life. Let me handle this weight for you. These people will be cursed with confusion simply because they don't understand why you died for them and refuse to *accept* your gift."

Yahshua replied, "Loving your neighbor as you love yourself can't be that hard to accept. Was it difficult for you to grasp that while you were in heaven?"

At this point, Yahshua decided to ignore the little devil and return to praying. Satan was once again stunned and confused by what Yahshua said. He witnessed my Lord stand his ground and not make a run for it using His power. He began to pray for the criminals across the hallway, specifically Kanaar, Jonarbi, and Barabbas. The criminals were awake, and heard every word. He continued to pray for all the criminals and guards in the prison, one by one, stating all of their names individually. Yahshua knew the hour had come and the flogging would soon begin, so He prayed without ceasing. God's voice continued to repeat the same orders. The heavenly Father told me to focus my attention on the other two criminals.

Soon after the words of God were spoken, the guards came to get Yahshua to take him away. An hour or so after Yahshua left, they took Kanaar. Soon after Kanaar left the cell, they took Jonarbi. God's voice gave me an update shortly afterwards. I was instructed to simply watch the men. First I watched the guards put the men into different chains. These chains were attached to the whipping posts. One of the commanders — the one Kanaar robbed — was given the opportunity to participate in the scourging. Lucretius, the centurion, and his fellow guards received the orders to begin. They engaged in the beating one by one.

The highest ranking official within the arena styled area sat off to the side while the crowd watched the violence. Kanaar could no longer keep his composure when the flogging focused on his rib cage. The whippings became more gruesome and ruthless. Blood spilled and squirted onto the ground. Kanaar yelled in agony until he no longer had the energy to yell. His entire backside was bruised, bloodied, and deeply slashed by the bones of the whips. His broken arm was not spared from the cracking weapons of death. Once they were finished, they dragged him back into the same cell in the prison he stayed the night before. They didn't bother to put him into shackles. They simply closed the door behind him.

I went back to see Jonarbi. I witnessed him cry out to his wife once he saw her in the crowd. She stood in tears as the men picked up different tools of torture. He tried to hold back the yelling but his groans grew louder and louder. The soldiers picked up a different weapon and initiated more beatings across Jonarbi's back. As the blood spilled and hit the ground, so did his wife's heart. She could no longer bear the sight of him like that. She cried out Jonarbi's name, and fled from the arena. He saw her leave and a part of his will to withstand the pain left as well. He screamed in terror as the bones went deeper and deeper into his back, hamstrings, and calf muscles. When they were tired and Jonarbi seemed to go into shock, the men were ordered to stop and take Jonarbi back into the prison. I followed the guards as they dragged Jonarbi's limp body.

CHAPTER FOURTEEN

The two thieves groaned in agony and could barely move due to the pain. The other three angels looked upon them with pity. Barabbas remained standing upright in shackles. He didn't have much to say. He stood there and shook his head at what he saw. I still did not like that man. All of his words and actions were filled with the worst intentions. The voice of God penetrated my spirit. He said that I should allow Barabbas to leave. I did not understand what it meant at first, but nevertheless I took heed.

"Those Roman bastards did this?" Barabbas said with disgust.

The wounded men attempted to sit upright. They looked at each other, surprised that either made it this far. One of them asked the other if he had overheard the other guards talk about Yahshua and his whereabouts. The other criminal did not have any knowledge, and he did not seem to be concerned. All three of the criminals were suddenly frightened when a few guards abruptly appeared. Looking directly at Barabbas, they opened the door and two of the soldiers reached for the shackles that held his wrists. Another guard reached for the chains on his waist.

"Alright, you are coming with us," one of the guards stated.

"What have I done?" Barabbas asked.

"Pontius Pilate wants to see you. He is going to ask the angry mob out there who will be set free, you or Yahshua."

"My sweet victory has finally arrived! If the guards that were here last night have any input on Yahshua's fate, I will be free. I won't stay to watch you two die so I bid you both farewells."

Kanaar said, "Wait! You cannot be serious. He killed a man in cold blood but you are going to let him free? Why do we still have to die for what we have done? This is an outrage!"

"Don't be so jealous, Kanaar. If you killed that family instead of just robbing them, you would have had a fifty-fifty chance of being free. I am lucky, that is it."

Jonarbi spat at him, "You jackal."

"You shouldn't be so concerned and heavy-hearted Jonarbi. I hear there is a recently widowed mother of a few children that stays around the west area, if I'm not mistaken. I should pay them all a visit and give my condolences."

"You wouldn't dare. You stay away from my family! You hear me? Stay away from my family!"

The guards yanked Barabbas out of the prison cell escorting him down the hallway to freedom. I hoped he was lying. Those are not the words you say to someone who is at their lowest. Jonarbi continued to yell hysterically towards Barabbas after he left. One of the guards returned to kick Jonarbi in the middle of his chest. That indeed silenced him for the moment, as he squirmed and struggled to regain his breath.

It did not take long for more soldiers to return for the two criminals. They took them outside, in the middle of the angry mob. People were shouting and spitting on them. There were some that even threw rocks at their heads. It was painful to watch the soldiers totally disregard the condition of Kanaar's arm when they tied it to the wooden beam that he would die upon. Jonarbi was overcome with grief about everything as he stood there in pain. However, throughout this process I noticed that one of the criminals actively watched Yahshua while He carried His cross in front of them. Although the sacrificial lamb currently had some clothes on his back, the thief saw the blood that soaked His garments, the bloody hair and face. I witnessed him look at Yahshua's lower legs and feet. They were all covered with blood. One of the men robbed the holy temple, and another attacked someone's household. I cannot say that either received forgiveness from the ones they attacked that day, yet one of them remained *focused* on Yahshua.

As they walked towards Golgotha's hill, a Roman soldier yelled to the crowd, "You there! Come forward and help Yahshua."

"Me?" the man asked.

"Yes. What is your name?"

The man looked to his left and his right and noticed that men and women moved away from him. Some of the men that once stood close by hid behind the crowd to avoid being seen by the guard. He stepped forward while walking over the rocks that were thrown at the rugged cross. He looked upon Yahshua with confusion because he didn't know what to make of Him.

"My name is Simon, from Cyrene."

"Simon, help this man."

Simon struggled to carry his end of the weight. His hands slid on the bloody cross and dropped it completely when Yahshua stumbled and fell. Simon reached down and gave a helping hand. Christ's grip was strong and he put forth His best effort to stand. He never said a word to Simon, but He nodded His head in gratitude. Once they reached the top of the hill, Simon let the cross down and looked upon Christ's face. His heart dropped to his stomach. The guards came over and forced Simon away from Christ while he wept bitterly.

The Roman soldiers held Yahshua down as they nailed spikes through His hands and feet at nine in the morning. The men hung Yahshua high and stretched him wide. The other two criminals received similar treatment. High priests, Romans, and the Jews mocked and spat at all of them.

The sky had become completely dark at noon when one of the criminals said to the other two men, "Look above your heads. Even the gods poured their anger onto the skies. There is no hope for us."

All the while, the other thief completely ignored the sky. His sights were set on Christ. That one criminal continued to stare at the man in the center. I couldn't put my finger on it, but it looked like he was patiently waiting for Yahshua to respond to all that had happened.

Yahshua said, "Father, forgive them, for they do not know what they do."[3]

As the Roman officials divided up His clothes by casting lots, the criminal heard His words and his eyes began to water. He slowly closed his eyes while a single tear fell down his face. Something was going on here. I'm not certain what this criminal was thinking about. The other criminal heard these words as well and I saw him look at Yahshua, but everything about this thief's composure remained unchanged.

CHAPTER FIFTEEN

The three assigned angels and I couldn't do much of anything at this point. Ironically, I attend executions frequently but I felt a lot of discomfort watching this one. Yahshua was in so much pain, yet He remained focused and put His energy towards praying for the people that were there to witness, including His disciples and His mother. I could only join my entourage in prayer as we hovered above the crowd. We were waiting for something that would turn this shameful display of mankind upside down.

"You are all fools with wings! There is no stopping this. Can Yahshua touch and heal himself while being nailed on the cross? No. Can he touch and heal the other two men while being nailed to a cross? No. Give it a rest. There's no hope," Satan shouted to us.

One of Satan's brothers added, "These men are doomed. Who in their right minds will believe in a King of Kings while he is dying in the midst of the worst criminals? Yahshua will be seen as guilty. No men who hear of this day will believe that Yahshua has done anything for their soul because of this. His life is ending because men are killing him. Why would anyone want to associate themselves with that? Men and women alike will turn their backs on their own people and forget about them. It is in their nature to hate one another. All it takes is a few woeful marks in their past. It is so simple. I know you understand this, so why don't you *accept* this?"

"One man is an outcast and no one from his family has come to witness his execution. The other man's wife and children are too ashamed to show their faces here. These men will die alone and burn alone," a devil's advocate stated.

Another demon shouted, "Look at them, it is pathetic. The man on the left cannot stand himself. He is squirming and shaking a little bit up there. Surely he will be with us soon."

Suddenly I heard a loud voice that made my chest tremble; it said *"watch him."*

I received my orders so I gave both bandits my undivided attention. Their blood slowly trickled down their crosses. The criminals groaned in pain and readjusted their bodies to breathe, making the pain worse. They were struggling to stay alive while the rulers, soldiers, citizens, and the rest of the crowd mocked Yahshua.

Suddenly, of one of the condemned spoke, "If You are Yahshua, save Yourself and us!"[4]

But the other criminal rebuked him. "Do you not even fear God," he said, "seeing you are under the same condemnation? And we indeed justly, for we receive the due reward of our deeds; but this Man has done nothing wrong." Then he said, "Lord, remember me when You come into Your kingdom."[5]

Yahshua answered him, "Assuredly, I say to you, today you will be with Me in Paradise."[6]

"Hallelujah, glory to God Almighty!" one of the angels shouted.

Another angel shouted, "Praise His holy name! Yahshua!"

A third angel was filled with so much joy that he couldn't fully pronounce his words. He was ecstatic and his voice joined all of those angels looking down from heaven, for they were also a cloud of witnesses to what had been said by the criminal and by Yahshua. The evil spirit left that criminal's body. The angel knew his brothers and the Most High were watching and had seen everything. He wanted to join them with song and dance. With a loud yell, the angel spread his wings and took off into the air. His wings moved with so much power and force he vanished from my sight quickly.

As I thanked God and praised Yahshua for saving the criminal, Satan yelled, "No. No. No. No! No! AAHHH! This is impossible!"

"You failed. Yahshua is victorious, yet again. He has taken your efforts to defeat Him and remained the same," I told him.

With a disgruntled look upon his face, he turned around to face me and said, "This isn't over yet. That man will crumble underneath some pressure, they all do. You'll see."

With his efforts in a scramble, Satan attempted to regain his footing after the blow. He didn't know exactly how to recover from Yahshua remaining the same. More shockingly, he did not know how Christ was able to give a soul eternal life while simultaneously being in the process of dying. Satan called a few demons over to help him out, and instructed his followers to harden the other robber's heart, and influence him to become bitter and suspicious of what had happened. Satan ultimately wanted the criminal to lose faith in this paradise Yahshua spoke of before he took his last breath. So they began to play on the skeptical criminal's emotions and filled his mind with negative thoughts. These thoughts unfortunately tricked the man to believe in his own foolishness, and it put the kind of hatred in his heart that would cause him to reject anything that was good. The man's ears became spiritually closed off and useless.

"Thank God," the criminal said, while gasping for air.

The criminal on the other side of Yahshua said, "Do you really believe this man? He already got beaten worse than we did. He is delusional."

"Control your tongue! Yes I believe in Yahshua. Who else could be so willing to forgive me? He had to be sent from the real God up there. He accepted my plea for salvation as if He knew me my whole life and was patiently waiting for me to come around."

"It is too good to be true. Do you think Yahshua truly knows what you have done? How can you be so sure since this is the closest you've ever gotten to this condemned man?"

"My entire life I've been searching for something or someone to accept me as I am and show compassion. Yes I admit I did live on a different path. I looked at other gods and wondered if they were real. When I wasn't doing that, I tried to ease the discomfort of not knowing the true God by simply living aimlessly day to day, going through the motions just to get by. The worst thing I've ever done was stealing. Yet I never met anyone who could blindly and with authority ask God for forgiveness for so many people. I felt the urge and the courage to ask this man for forgiveness, even though I'm not worth it. I'm not sure if I would forgive me if the tables were turned and I was the one who was robbed."

"You are going to believe that after we die *we* are going to paradise?!?! Were you born yesterday? You and I are going to die and will not be buried. We will be feasted on by the beasts and the birds that smell our cooling bodies. These Roman and Jewish jackals will burn whatever is left of us after nature is full and no longer desires us. I bet they will set our remaining flesh on fire while our bodies remain hanging."

"Yahshua also gave me *hope* for the future that is past my rotting corpse. I believe that when he said 'forgive them' that I am a part of the 'them' Yahshua is referring to."

"You sound ridiculous and I am beyond vexed at this point. You are going to burn or go to a place filled with emptiness like everybody else when they die. Unfortunately, we are going to hell! You will be no better off than me. What about our talk that we had less than a day ago?"

"In all fairness, Yahshua looked towards me and told me I'm going to paradise after pleading for Him to *remember me*. I didn't know that would happen, but I genuinely asked Him for forgiveness with all my heart and all that I could muster. Therefore, yesterday and any day before no longer matters…especially now that I am paying the price for those actions! Unfortunately, *Christ did not say anything good will happen to you because you would rather sulk in pride than ask Him for forgiveness.* I'm no better than you are in any form or fashion, yet deep down I know I need something so pure that it's undeserved and seemingly out of reach. Why don't you just ask Yahshua? In a strange way, you are being selfish. I know you can't give your guilt and shame to me or anyone else. Yet the one person who can get rid of that trouble is the man you scoff at."

One of my brothers stood guard and protected the criminal that believed in Yahshua. He kept careful watch at what was taking place. He walked in random sequence around the criminal, pacing consistently back and forth. All the while, he was praising God for bringing this man's soul into the great number in the heavens. The other angel laid his hands on his chest and shoulder and he prayed over the criminal, not stopping.

The other criminal chimed in, "It's so obvious. He did something to be put up here in the first place. He needs forgiveness just as much as we do. Look at the crowd. Aren't they all such great people? The soldiers, the ones who should be the outstanding citizens, are engaging in illegal activity by gambling right in front of the so-called Son of God. Are these upholders of the law gambling over the clothes of Yahshua? Why would the real living God allow this to happen to His son? I can tell you why, because he is weak like us and truly isn't sent from some sort of paradise."

"Quiet or I'll stab you with my spear!" the centurion yelled.

"You must look at the world in how Yahshua treats those that are in it. Yes, the soldier is not the best example of great living, and we aren't ether. Yahshua is here on a cross regardless if we believe Him or not. He is here. However, He treats us the way we would like to be treated, and even better than we could imagine."

"What are you talking about?"

"In spite of how the centurion is treating Yahshua and how he is acting in front of Yahshua, He has not said anything out of retaliation. I'm not a wise man, but I would say that any of us: us robbers, the townspeople, and the soldiers would say something if we were in His sandals. It would be well deserved and no one would blame that person for doing so. However, He is praying not only for the same gambler, but for everyone around. Yahshua cannot be one of us. He has to be from the real God."

Lucretius interjected, "That's enough. I can break your legs right now so don't tempt me."

"Yahshua has to have great power, a power that none of us understand, to not only pray for another person's forgiveness in spite of things, but to give something undeserved and precious as *refuge in times of trouble, especially now that I brought destruction on my own life*. If this centurion came searching for something or someone as humbly as I did and heard of Yahshua, He would have compassion for him. Because of his faith, simply touching His clothes would heal him or give the centurion peace for whatever burden he carried."

"I'll make a wager that this will shut your mouth!" the centurion yelled while reaching for his club.

"Christ didn't take me down from the cross, but he *saved* me from sinking after my death. My faith allowed Yahshua to carry my heavy debt of sin after my death. Now, these inward thoughts of death are lighter, because Yahshua will take me to a high place when this is over. Since the centurion has no faith in Him and no recognition of who Yahshua is, he simply is touching clothes that he won in gambling. Nothing more or less will happen. After I am dead and gone, and when I'm off to paradise, he will return home with the same problems that he came here with."

I stood there in awe as I watched Lucretius' reaction. His shoulders slumped a little bit and the glare in his eyes eased up. He dropped the club which he truly intended to use. His emotions were running high until the criminal had said those words. Now he had slowed down. Lucretius stopped gambling and walked away from the clothes on the ground, including the pieces that he won. Lucretius stood back to take in everything that was going on. He stood there to be alone with his thoughts. Meanwhile, Kanaar and Jonarbi continued to go back on forth with the few breaths of air that they had left. From time to time they would both stop because of the pain, but one seemed to have caught his second wind as he hung high.

"There is no point in believing in this hocus-pocus. Yahshua is in the same predicament that we are in. The people around us are taking shots at us for sport. Yet somehow, you're saying the man hanging next to us is some of savior?"

"Mind your tongue! He's my savior. You are focusing on people that can point arrows with their words. Yet, it is always in our nature to frown upon something and take its splendor. Only the *righteous* can give. Yahshua is somehow with us to give us forgiveness. Ask Him for it."

"But I do not understand so I can't accept it just yet. How come these people are hurling insults at us when we are at their lowest and go unaccountable for their actions, yet we are the only ones dying on the cross for our judgment? This is just not fair. This life that god of yours created isn't fair."

"I can't argue that. Life isn't fair. These people need forgiveness for their wrongdoings just as much as we do, yet they are not suffering with an instant consequence. On top of that, we saw a mass murderer, who should already be dead because of his notorious acts, be set free from prison because a coward in ruler's attire decided to let him go unharmed. Surely Pontius Pilate had his reasons to let Barabbas go instead of Yahshua. I cannot tell you why some men live to do wrong, some men die because of others doing wrong, or why no one wants to even strive to be right. But I can tell you one thing…"

"Is that so? What is your great wisdom my conniving brethren?"

"Stop looking at the men and women around you. You are only using them as an excuse to justify yourself in not believing in the true and living God. Yahshua is here in our midst because He was sent from God. Now whether you believe it or not, if you are in a situation that you would pay the ultimate price or get away free, on the cross next to Him or the man mocking Him, the loved one weeping for His wounds or the believer that is not here to witness it, you are still faced with the same decision. You are going to have to make up your mind: are you going to believe in Yahshua and his power, or will you reject it?!"

"No I just, I just, don't understand…"

"I choose to believe, not knowing anything about much of anything else. All I know is guilt, loneliness, and especially shame. I am tired of holding on to the shame of what has brought me here on the cross in the first place. Even now, I refuse to hold on to the shame that the witnesses here right now give me. I will no longer hold on to the guilt that the witnesses gave when they caught me doing the crime. I just can't take it anymore, but Yahshua can. He is the only one who can take this beating and still show love. I don't know why Yahshua is like this but He is for all of us."

"You sound like one of those crazy religious fanatics. You wouldn't know the real god from your right or left hand."

"Both of my hands are nailed like yours you fool! Stop wasting the little time you have with me and talk to Him!"

The condemned man was holding strong. I was greatly pleased by this. I could see his sustained injuries but he was feeling a source of power. He was not necessarily given a rush through his veins by all of this, but something that runs much deeper. Perhaps, he was feeling a warming sensation in his heart. This man had *conviction*, and it was carrying him through all the pain that he was enduring. The most astonishing thing is that the angel wasn't taking his pain away. On the contrary, the angel was praying for him to endure the pain. Although it hurt to breathe, the angel was praying for the criminal to have courage to not only continue to breathe and endure more struggle, but to use his efforts to speak to the other criminal's soul.

Now the sixth hour had come. It was dark and a lot of the crowd had walked away to retire for the evening. I gazed upon the condemned criminals and they looked exhausted yet their struggle was not complete, not yet. My eyes saw Yahshua and He tilted His head, almost by coincidence, towards my direction. With conviction I now could reaffirm the difference between understanding life and death and accepting the one who controls both. The truth was that understanding and accepting are two totally different things.

Later, knowing that everything had now been finished, so that Scripture would be fulfilled, Yahshua said, "I thirst."[7]

Maybe His mouth was dry and He needed a drink of water. Could anyone blame Yahshua for making such a request at a time like that? I couldn't imagine being in that situation, and my heart fell to the ground when I look at Him. Could anyone imagine calling out to one of their best friends as a betrayer, and witness it come to pass in the next few hours?

Could anyone imagine their friend pledging his allegiance to always be by someone's side, but they saw the friend deny knowing their existence three times? Could anyone imagine that a friend would commit suicide the day after they saw him? I can't imagine the vanity Christ was faced with once he received the news. Yahshua was going to die for their sins. Couldn't Judas hold on for just a little while longer? That shame and wretchedness was not meant for Judas to carry at all. It is hard for me to imagine that pain, being an angel. Unfortunately, the mental weight that Christ could bear was put to the test because all of these things happened within twenty-four hours. Nevertheless, Yahshua remained vigilant to carry out God's will and offer His body as a sacrifice for these same people. His only request was so simple.

A soldier went over and took a sponge and dunked it into a container filled with sour wine. That caught the attention of Jonarbi, since he recognized the color of the liquid. The man shoved the sponge onto the end of a spear and raised the sponge toward Yahshua. If he could bite down on the sponge, Yahshua would be able to draw fluid. Strangely enough, after He tasted what was in the sponge, Yahshua denied the drink.

What was wrong with the drink? Was it poisoned? Was the taste of the drink displeasing? Jonarbi stared at him, waiting for a response, yet Yahshua did not give any. Jonarbi drank wine all the time, especially after a hard day's work. That would be a relief to anyone in his shoes to get that for a drink. I paused to think. Yahshua never had a problem with drinking alcohol. He simply never drank in excess. The first miracle He performed was turning water into wine at a wedding. Just yesterday, He drank wine and ate bread with His disciples.

When I remember what He had done in the past, the drinks were because of a joyous occasion or celebration; meals; ceremonies, remembering the past, fellowship, love, and friendship. So perhaps,

Yahshua refused the drink because He wanted to honor all of these things. But Yahshua knew the pasts of Jonarbi and Kanaar and knew that they've handled their indulgences improperly. Christ refused drink to show them self-control. It would've been hard for Christ to show them this if he had one small drink during this terrible hour. That single drink during His crucifixion could have been misconstrued, letting the masses know it is fine to drink through their issues.

Nevertheless Yahshua was dying on the cross to fulfill the word of God and scriptures written previous to His birth. He was on a mission. Although Yahshua was working extremely hard for man's benefit, that wasn't time to search for a temporary relief, or a drink to take the edge off. He had come to take everyone's pain, sufferings, guilt, and shame without a murmuring word.

When he had received the drink, Yahshua yelled, "It is finished." And bowing His head, He gave up His spirit.[8]

Then Lucretius, seeing what had happened, praised God and said, "Certainly this was a righteous Man!"[9]

Both thieves were in awe. Both men's hearts began to beat rapidly as they hung. The Jewish community did not want the crucifixion to continue past dark, so the soldiers took heed to break their legs. The men knew that the end was near. With a big grunt, the soldier swung his club into the legs of the first criminal who Christ said would join him in paradise. Soon after his legs were broken, I ran over to release the angel who prayed and laid hands on the hanging body. There was no need for him to suffer any longer. For a first time in a long time I felt compassion for a man, and I did not want to do my job anymore. I knew he was covered by Christ's blood. He struggled enough in this life, and he didn't need to struggle anymore. My heavenly Father finally revealed the meaning to my assignment, and He gave me the permission to perform my duty. When I laid my hands on him he immediately relaxed and stopped breathing.

I walked over to the other criminal as the soldier swung his club towards the limbs. I wanted to end the suffering of this criminal as well, but a burning chill gave me pause. What if the criminal still needs more time? I know God told me to take his life too and the time has come for me to do so, yet I paused. I could only wish that the man had more time, but how much time does one need to make up their mind to what they believe? I was glad I did not plan the details of that, but I had to do what was necessary. When the criminal struggled to use his legs for another breath, I let him struggle for a moment. At that point, what was done was done and I made up my mind that I did want not to delay. I laid my hands on this condemned soul, and the body ceased to move.

CHAPTER SIXTEEN

The Bible says, "Then, behold, the veil of the temple was torn in two from top to bottom; and the earth quaked, and the rocks were split, and the graves were opened; and many bodies of the saints who had fallen asleep <u>were raised</u>; and coming out of the graves after His resurrection, they went into the holy city and appeared to many."[10]

I added more to the scroll's account of these events as the remaining witnesses to the crucifixion wept over Christ's body. Soon I began to see bright lights from up above. There were my brothers, many of them, descending from the heavens through the sky. They held many believers that passed away. They all were smiling and filled with excitement. My brothers were in numbers so large that they appeared as numerous as the stars. They flew down with the souls of believers. Some of them came down not far away from the hill of Golgotha, directly towards graves. The wings of my brothers quickened and the old souls were put back into the tomb.

As I marveled in what I saw, an angel holding an old soul that I delivered to the Father many days ago came to me. As the angel landed, the old man walked towards me, in front of the body of Christ. He covered his mouth and a tear rolled down his face. He bowed down to his slain master out of respect.

When the man stood up he said in bold fashion, "Hello, my friend."

"Friend? I don't have many of those," I replied.

"Well, now you have one in me."

"Those words are music to my ears," I replied. "What did you see from up above?"

With great enthusiasm the old man said, "I've seen it all. Everything was revealed to me. I've seen the Holy Spirit working on my behalf when I lifted my hands and praised God. When I wasn't sure what to do and prayed; I saw angels sent to my aid. So many times when I made mistakes in my life, I saw the Lord forgive me, and never mention the sin again. When I entered into my new home I was welcomed by my ancestors and angels and angelic beings that I could never have imagined. It was beautiful."

"Have you witnessed what has happened on earth?"

"Yes. All of us were focused on Golgotha. No one had ever seen such a great sacrifice. After Yahshua died and the earth shook, I saw the veil of the temple where I used to worship being ripped apart from top to bottom. Yet the guards are blind to who He is. They only cared that Yahshua was dead and pierced His side to make sure the deed was complete."

"Now that your body will be raised back to life, where are you going to worship and disciple others?"

"You know, I haven't put much thought into the building itself. Surely, I would want to enter the temple to which I was accustomed, but it is currently ruined. They could rebuild it or move elsewhere and I can follow. But wherever I go, I want to be where they speak freely about the works of Christ. If it wasn't for Him, I wouldn't have been brought back to life in the first place."

"How are you going to live this life if you wake up and cannot remember anything? What are you going to do in your life if you cannot remember anything from your first judgement day?"

"Now that, my friend, I can answer without hesitation. I will remember who gives me life and exalt His praises everywhere all of the days of my life. I cannot focus on my second death any more than I could on my first one. Even though I may appear to be awkward to old friends, loved ones, and complete strangers, I shall stay that course."

"That is good to hear."

"In the meantime, I am excited to see my wife again. She is still mourning and she has not remarried. I will be glad to comfort her once again."

"I understand. I know it was sudden once I appeared, but I've done all I could to make your transition as…"

"Be still, my friend. No need to apologize for doing God's will, even if it ruffles the feathers of a few saints and angels alike."

"You must go now. Be the man God wants you to be. Be the provider for your family, the priest of your household, and…"

"My wife's protector and shield from danger. It is time to shake the dust off and tie the straps of my sandals once again. Do me a favor, can you talk with our heavenly Father about my second death. If it is in His will, is it possible to…"

"Die in the same fashion or along with your wife? I'll make a request on your behalf. After all, we are here to serve you. Until we meet again, go in peace."

He bowed and made a vow that he would not fear death anymore, for he found a friend and new meaning from me. The angel standing next to him took hold of his hand and left to go to his burial grounds. Above my head was a great multitude of brothers with saints from all around the land. I only wished that Christ's mother and His disciples and the centurion could see what I saw.

There was one brother, however, who stood far above the rest. He remained firmly on the clouds of heaven holding a baby. When he attempted to fly down to earth, the baby cried loudly. A few times, Gabriel tried to calm the baby unsuccessfully. After his last attempt, he paid close attention to the baby as he landed and stood still. The baby lifted her little hands towards the gates. Her eyes never left from God's presence and the baby did not want to leave or go any farther.

"Be still. The little one has made her decision," God told Gabriel.

Gabriel tried his best to remain militant, but he could not help but feel tears running down his face. Tears of joy, tears of hope, and tears of his heart's contentment gave him comfort. He stood there watching everything happen, awaiting my arrival with the two thieves. That is when I realized I must finish the work God has given me.

CHAPTER SEVENTEEN

"For no other foundation can anyone lay than that which is laid, which is Jesus Christ. Now if anyone builds on this foundation with gold, silver, precious stones, wood, hay, straw, each one's work will become clear; for the Day will declare it, because it will be revealed by fire; and the fire will test each one's work, of what sort it is. If anyone's work which he has built on it endures, he will receive a reward. If anyone's work is burned, he will suffer loss; but he himself will be saved, yet so as through fire."[111]

I was humbled by what God had shown me. Before my eyes Yahshua, God's living word, laid down His life not only for those two men, but for all who followed Him, even the ones who persecuted and cursed His name. Yahshua had done so much for them. He loved them so much, and so deeply I cannot count or begin to fathom how to measure it. Being one of His angels, I finally was able to see the Planner's will come to pass. Only at this point, I started to not only hear the words but saw the actions that words could not explain. Although it wasn't the first time I had done this, I fell to my knees and covered my eyes with my wings while facing Christ. I felt warming sensations around my head that I knew only came from above.

I called on his name "Yahshua, the Son of God."

I lifted my head and looked the Messiah in His eyes. His spirit was before me. My master's smile slowly started to fade, and then disappeared. I looked upon His body and praised God for sending Him because only He could have taken a beating like that for someone else. I then gazed upon the men to his right and left.

With new perspective, I said, "Come out."

As both of them stepped out of their physical bodies onto the ground, one asked, "What is going on? Are those angels soaring in the air?"

"Do not be afraid, for this suffering is over now. Come with me, for the heavenly Father knew this day and hour was coming, and we are right on schedule. This is a great day, for today you are both going to meet God face-to-face."

"Which god are we going to? I have never seen or experienced him before. I cannot tell the difference between any of them," the man on the left stated.

With a renewed compassion, even for his predicament, I responded, "I will tell you the truth. You have suffered a terrible struggle being crucified and your head may be still ringing. I come to bring you before the man that can renew all things! He is the reason why everyone has life. If you think I'm bright and shiny, wait until you see His overpowering presence and His face! He chooses not to reveal it to anyone until the time when He calls His children home. However, Yahshua is His son. He sent Him down here to meet you and all His people in person. You were blessed to meet Him in the flesh for a few hours. Surely you two will recognize each other in His kingdom."

"Yes I guess so, that being the case. He will remember me because he knows how much pain I endured and how distraught I was."

"Well then, now is the time. Let's go to see the heavenly Father. Let's go."

With desperation the other man's soul cried out, "But where is He? *His word is all I have, and all I have to show for my life!* I have to see Him. Why isn't He here with us? He died shortly before the Roman soldiers broken our legs. He said I would be in paradise with Him. If I was still alive, I would've done things differently. I probably still have my faults but I wouldn't be too proud to ask for forgiveness, the same way I did on the cross. I think Yahshua was going to vouch for me. If I can only stand before Him with you to say that He genuinely had all of my hope, you would understand my plea. He has to remember me, for my sake. He didn't have to, but He said..."

"Do not be afraid, for His word is God's will! He commands His own spirit to arise, to come and to go as He pleases. The man you met gives me orders to bring your spirits out of your worldly vessels. His spirit is alive and well, indeed."

"Then why isn't Yahshua's spirit here with us? It was only a moment later that we passed away?"

"He is fulfilling your promise! Praise God. He told you that He will meet you in paradise, so He had to leave you here, only for a moment. He has gone to personally write your name in the Book of Life, the list of reservations for those that will be joining Him in heaven. If Yahshua said that you are going to meet Him in paradise, you're free indeed. He left to prepare a special place for you in His heavenly kingdom. He is waiting patiently for us to meet Him there so we can adore Him once again and experience the true bliss of God's splendor."

"Let's go!"

I reached out my left and right hands for them to grab. Once they took hold, I immediately clinched to have a firm grip. My wings flapped to leave the ground once again, to take a familiar route to the great I AM. I knew He was waiting patiently. I know God does not expect me to be late, but I wonder if He knows that I may be arriving early in spirit. I forced my wings to accelerate us as quickly as possible. As we began to leave the Earth's atmosphere, I started to really pick up speed.

The devil was a sore loser. So Satan and a few demons followed behind me, to get a glimpse as to what would happen on the two criminals' Day of Judgment. The soul on my right was relieved, blessed, and renewed with a spirit of anticipation and expectancy, even after his death! He was truly in for a great sight.

"My Lord, I have returned with the two men you've requested," I said humbly on a bended knee.

"Well done. Gabriel, you stay with the one on the left. I want to see the other man first. Bring him forward," God ordered.

"Yes, my Lord," I answered. "Where do want us to stand?"

"Bring the man ten paces in front of the gate, but do not enter the gates."

I walked calmly with the man to the correct area. It wasn't necessary for the other criminal to feel nervous or upset, so Gabriel did his best to hold a small conversation with him while still holding the small baby. The man who had received Christ's grace had many questions about what was happening and what was going to occur, so he answered them without referring to the other being judged. My heavenly Father leaned forward upon His throne so the man beside me could see His face.

My Father said, "I've waited for this moment for a long time. Are you alright?"

"Yes," the man replied in a distressed tone.

"Good. We shall begin to review your days."

The man stood in disbelief as everything was shown, no detail was missed. From birth he saw every moment and thought until his execution. When he wanted to give explanations for everything, he found himself unable to give a straight answer for his actions. He struggled at providing his account during the end of his life. My Lord was deeply concerned about when the man hung on the cross next to Christ.

God asked, "Why do you believe that I treated you unfairly?"

The man replied, "I died the worst death possible when I did not commit the worst crime. I did not get a second chance or mercy like everyone else at Golgotha."

"Why is everyone else your concern? Do you understand the question that you ask? The men and women and children who lived and died before you stood before me. Every African, Asian, Roman, Greek, Jew, and Gentile will stand alone before my throne. So what is fair, and what is not fair?"

"Fair is when a wrongful deed is done, everyone will be held accountable. No one should be left out of the consequences."

"I see. Have you considered my Son?"

"Who is your son? When have I seen him?"

His lack of acknowledgement had created a growing frustration. I was not fond of the man's attitude or the responses to God's questions. Using my size and strength to my advantage, I stepped on the back of his leg, forcing the thief to kneel. Then his demise began to set in when his face was hard pressed against the floor. The tip of the sword tickled the back of his neck, demanding respect.

"Answer me. Who is my son?" God asked.

"Is it Yahshua?"

"Yes. Now, what do you think of my fairness towards my own son, whom I handed over to men to be unjustifiably crucified just so I could be *close* to you?"

"My God, oh God have mercy on me. I didn't know this truth... Please save me from my evil deeds. Haven't I suffered enough of your wrath?"

"My Wrath... Your poor soul crumbles under the wrath of men. Your eyes have not seen my fury, not yet."

"Your son, Yahshua, is the king of kings, lord over everything. He is full of mercy. Let Him speak on my behalf, I beg of you."

"He will."

As God leaned back on His thrown, Christ proclaimed His judgment, "I never knew you, and your name is not written in the Book of Life. Depart from me."

The man was in total denial and could not bear the words he heard, but how could he? The man never accepted Christ. The robber attempted to steal away from my grasp. He dug his fingertips into the floor and crawled towards the gate. He couldn't escape from under my foot. I picked him up by his wrists and began the journey far away from God's presence, away from the truth, away from the light. As I flew over the destitute horizon, the evil spirits cackled below.

"Look at this fool," Satan said to his fellow demons. "The man's kicking and screaming is our reward. He wags his head in all directions in desperation."

One of the devils added, "You were right, my lord. You said one would surely die. Only fire will give this man a warm welcome."

Once I returned from the empty abyss, the gates opened for me. Gabriel and the other thief were no longer standing outside. I walked along a path paved with gold and splendor, passing those who were full of cheer, laughter, song, and dance. As I approached my Father's heavenly throne, I saw Gabriel's head. Once I stood next to Gabriel I finally saw the man a few steps in front, kneeling. I didn't hear a sound as he held his face in his hands.

"I know this man and his name is written here," Yahshua said while pointing his finger in the Book of Life. "Father, you are with me and I'm in him."

A great voice added, "And I'm with him too."

My Lord stood up from the right hand of the Father. He walked down the steps of His glory, and approached the man. Gabriel and I took a knee out of respect. Yahshua laid his hand upon his shoulder and stated the criminal's name. The two stood as he watched his life before his eyes. The man gave an account for every moment, every thought, every action, every hour. I observed the Father and Son's reactions to the good things the man had done. Even when the man did not see an immediate result for the good deed given, they were pleased that the man made the best decision. Despite those previous circumstances, the Lord was glad to see him in this fashion.

"My servant, these deeds have rewarded you greatly. Great wealth and crowns await you. These are gifts from me and I want you to be steward of them," God stated.

I watched diligently when the man made bad decisions and committed sinful acts. The man gave his reasoning before the Father. The Father and Son did not dwell on these facts. Their conversation flowed effortlessly to the next moment in his life.

"My servant, look me in my eyes and answer me truthfully. Why have you chosen to seek me only *after* your circumstances changed for the worse?" our Father asked.

The man answered, "I wanted to pull myself out of the situation. I had too much pride to ask."

"So, did you control the favor that occurred in your life?"

"Well, no."

"So why would you try to think your hands were as powerful as mine?"

"Oh Father, must I give my honest..."

"Yes."

"At once I thought you existed because things were good in my life, or you gave me a blessing from a far, far distance away. Sometimes I thought it was pure chance that my hands had coins to provide for myself or being able to be content with a life not knowing you. When I walked, then ran further down the valley, I wanted to prove to myself that you did not exist. There were so many horrible things out of my control and it wasn't fair. Rage flowed through my soul. Out of spite I asked you 'God, how could you my allow life to be damned while I'm still alive' How could you let this happen?' and you never answered me. Why did you forsake me?"

"My son, I answered your prayers yet you *refused* to hear my answers, even in your dreams you hated me. I presented you a door that led to a longer life, yet you chose the way to your crucifixion. What prevented you from opening up to a new beginning?"

"My circumstances forced me to think of a hasty solution. I no longer wanted to struggle to rebuild or regain myself. I wanted out of my current life and there was no longer a cost I wasn't willing to pay."

"So this is why you put a wager on the trust of those who loved you? Did you ever love any of them?"

"My family and my friends, yes I loved them once. Yet I see the sacrifice your son has made for me. It was selfless and kind. I could never have done such a blind act for them, but I loved them. But when life was rough and jagged, they no longer saw my perspective. I was alone. They only looked at me as the one having a problem with no solutions. That is when my anger fought against them. My heart abandoned them in plain sight. I would've traded them all for being free of this burden."

God lifted his voice saying, "My servant, I am not like man, where revisiting a painful past would stir up anger towards another. Your sins are forgiven by my son but your crooked ways have forfeited all of these gifts, the heavenly treasures, and your crowns. You did not love one another as you loved yourself. Therefore, you will never see them for all eternity."

"My God, please! Do not forsake me," the man cried out. "My soul cannot take this penalty. I come to you with empty hands. There must be something I have done that was pleasing in your sight. How would your servant be a steward over nothing?"

I shouted, "There is one thing, my Lord, which is pleasing. You've seen the man. Please consider his last hours."

Gabriel and I watched along with the Father and Son. The stones and bones ripped through his flesh. Blood spilled everywhere. We all watched the man feel compassion when Yahshua was so weak that another man had to come to his side, carrying the cross to the hill. The nails were driven through the hands and feet. The man's attention was fixed upon Christ's glory. He silently wept when he heard the words, "forgive them."

The criminal watched his heart and thoughts changed drastically once He accepted Yahshua as Lord and Savior. He pushed himself past his bodily destruction and trusted his Lord's salvation. It didn't matter that other condemned man rebuked what he had to say. Nothing else mattered, nothing at all.

When I experienced viewing this moment for a second time, a warming sensation grew inside me and I could not deny its presence. Christ and our heavenly Father were pleased with what they saw, but they did not mention any rewards to be given to the man yet. Something must be said on this man's behalf.

As I stood up, I pleaded, "His actions are pure and it is your work completed Father! I have written it all down, everything. Am I not your humble servant? My hands have an account for all that he has done. It will last for all eternity, when earth is no more. Prove his work and make it pure. Bring fire to this holy scroll. Please, do not look past this man."

I walked towards the pedestal that holds the Book of Life. The stand was near the foot of the throne of God. As I walked, I felt the warming sensation surrounded me. I did not act in insubordination, but with purpose. It was only while walking in stride that I noticed how my Father's brightness increased with every step. His dazzling light was blinding, so I used one of my wings to block my eyes as a shield would. I got closer and closer, but my pace had slowed considerably because His presence pierced through my veil. With my eyes barely open, I could catch a glimpse of the precious book.

"If it takes me one thousand years to reach the foot of your throne, so be it. I'll prove to you that he is a righteous man, in your likeness. The Book of Life can withstand the flame. If this scroll can be sat upon the book and not be consumed, you can see that this man can be a steward of something in your kingdom," I said with confidence.

God smiled and said, "You will not have to reach the pedestal, for you have already proven this. Open your eyes and see this man's faith made pure."

My eyes were in awe at what I saw. The holy scroll glowed in uncontrollable waves. Flames encircled my entire body, the wings, my head, and down to the soles of my feet. I was amazed at what I saw. I cherished the moment. I fell to my knees and thanked God, for the thief was changed and shown approved. He didn't know the doctrine, the Torah, or memorization of scripture, yet his testimony of God's grace will last for all eternity! It will last longer than all things bound to earth.

The Holy Spirit spread throughout the heavens. As I looked around, everyone was engulfed in joy's heat, the smile I couldn't resist, the peace God shared, the blood Yahshua shed. We were all filled with praise of what was done. Through this man, God had shown that any past could be forgiven and forgotten. Only through Him, and only with Him this could exist. I only wished the men and women and children whom I casted down as dry sticks could have accepted Yahshua for themselves. The criminal and Christ prayed and offered praise to God.

At once God's voice spoke, "Your life has let the world hear of the good news, who that hears the word of God and accepts his gift of salvation will last until the end of days. Well done, my good and faithful servant. Surely what you've done on earth has rewarded you with treasures beyond your thoughts and your mind. I am the God of life everlasting. There is no man, no deterioration, nor hateful spirit who could steal this away from you!"

"Come this way. You have a great family waiting for you at the door of your new home. God answered their prayers and brought you to them. Even though you don't know them, they've prayed and labored for so long, requesting Him to honor this moment. Our Lord had blessed them beyond measure and given them the honor of presenting your crowns to you. God be praised!" Gabriel told the man.

"You two go forward. My Father has chosen not to resurrect your body, my friend," Yahshua explained. "The world will not even know your name. However, the God you served will raise my body from the grave, so everyone can believe. The same way you believed will be the same passion they will share. I will return soon, I promise."

Time had passed and Christ's time had drawn near. After He told the saved man the wonderful news, Yahshua left their presence. Gabriel and the man were left with smiles and filled with joy that could not be measured. I stayed to pray over my completed work. As I clutched the scroll, I walked towards the pedestal which held the Book of Life. I sat my holy scroll next to the foot of the post. The task was finished, and I had grown with understanding, and I only prayed for my Father's approval. Once I returned to a bended knee in front of the throne of the heavenly Father, He told me, "Well done, my good and faithful servant. Now then, there is another one I want to meet now. Are you ready for your next assignment?"

AFTERWORD

To keep the integrity of the Bible intact, the story ends without the thief's name revealed. Just like the word of God, we could only imagine how God's mercy can extend to men just like these. Accepting the Father's grace and mercy looks to be so easy, so simple. Yet how would you feel if you were on the receiving end of either Jonarbi's or Kanaar's crime? Sometimes we are robbed by familiar faces and we may feel more willing to give them forgiveness and a second chance. Are we comfortable giving the same forgiveness when our lives cross paths with people with no names or unrecognizable faces?

During my undergrad years on Mercer University's campus, I walked outside the student center to go watch an on-campus activity. A friend of mine had secretly joined a Greek fraternity, and I wanted to attend the probate ceremony (for those who do not know, this is the formal unveiling of the new members of a fraternity/sorority). I sat my books down near a bench and stood close by and glanced at them periodically as I watched my friend. After the ceremony had ended and I quickly congratulated my friend, I went back to the bench to get my books. They were gone.

I had back tracked my steps multiple times and came to the conclusion that someone stole my books. I was deeply upset. I was taking a 19 hour course load that semester, and I was using all of my books earlier that night to catch up in my studies. Those preowned books cost a total over $1000. I know what you are thinking- a thousand dollars is not what it used to be. To a broke college student, however, it felt like the world has officially turned its back on me. I needed to act fast. That night, I sent a mass email to the student body stating that my books were stolen with my contact information in case someone who knew where the books were. The next morning, I went to the bookstore and notified the person in charge at the opening hour. I gave them a list of the books that went missing along with my name and cell phone number.

Long story short, I retrieved all of the books since the thief attempted to get "a refund" for the stolen items at the campus book store. Interestingly enough, I was contacted by the person who took the books when I already had them back in my possession. After thinking about it for a minute, praying for another minute, I decided to meet this person face-to-face. This girl explained the whole story. It turns out that she planned the whole thing and had her gullible and naïve friend to take the books to the bookstore in an attempt to get a refund for the books she stole. I'm telling you the truth, the two robbers that entered my life appeared to be two teenage girls. To add insult to injury, this lady couldn't tell me the legitimate reason as to why she did it, or truly admit she was wrong for doing so.

After hearing her story, I told her that what was done is done, and I would not harp on the issue. I wouldn't press charges. My books were returned and I still had enough time to prepare for my upcoming exam. I then asked if she ever thought about working part-time so she won't have to feel pressured to steal again. I must admit, I felt strange showing compassion while this conversation was happening. I even offered to put her in contact with people that could help her get a job. She told me she worked but would not tell me what she did specifically. I took it lightly, and walked out the room. It was a feeling that I did not understand. I thought I would've been really angry that the girl scoffed at a helping hand. Everything made me feel extremely peculiar, and I felt goofy showing her kindness.

Thinking back on this event, this was a tough decision to make. No one said forgiveness was easy, yet it is always encouraged. Unfortunately, if someone turned on the TV to watch the news, or read a paper, or witnessed first-hand family members "borrowing" money, or have heard of family members being used for money, that may be a time where something is taken and the victim will never get it back. Hey, it happens. It is still our responsibility to forgive them as Christians. It is a tough decision to make, but someone has to do it. If the spirit of Christ truly dwells within us, we can pray and ask for the strength and the courage to do so.

Sometimes many parts of the Bible might be difficult to digest. Yet throughout the book, God shows that His power reigns high above man's capability. This power is so big that it's hard to explain. For example, if you were to read the story of Moses, God hardened Pharaoh's heart towards Moses. Every time he thought of letting the Hebrew slaves free, Pharaoh changed his mind and kept them in bondage. He fully did not change his mind until his son died of the final plague of Egypt. On the other hand, King Solomon (the assumed author of the book of Ecclesiastes) talked about the vanity in life, and pretty much complained about not understanding and not knowing the meaning of things. Nevertheless, he believed in God. Every time he thought of the goodness of God, he changed his mind and marveled at His ways. His faith in God kept him on the right path, even though the man did not see the point of anything. Surprisingly, God had blessed King Solomon with wisdom and he still didn't understand everything.

God has given the freedom of choice to everyone. Therefore, it is up to us what we choose with our free will and ultimately what character we will have. In my situation I have chosen to hold on to the faith in God that everything will be alright. When I feel the burden of my sins being lifted off my shoulders, I do not want to burden someone else by holding a huge grudge, even if they burdened me. We must continue to fight the good fight and run our race. Even if it hurts, when it is inconvenient, and there is no instant gratification we must remember how God showed His love for us when we hurt others and we did not believe in Jesus at one point in our life. In spite of it all, Jesus died for our sins and rose from the dead three days later to show His power (just like He predicted). That is an unimaginable amount of power!

People who are in prison need to be shown compassion and forgiveness — perhaps an extra dose of it. Salvation is not a light switch, something we can turn on and off at any time. We must remember we all have sinned against God and wronged our brother and sister. We should not try to hoard this gift of refuge to ourselves. This gift to share is for everyone. No excuses. If you have deep feelings that are keeping you from forgiving someone, do your best to pray and fast for God's peace immediately. Remember, like Jesus in the prison with criminals, you may be the closest encounter with God that they will ever have! We cannot blow this moment because of petty or dramatic situations since tomorrow is not promised. Of course, this is easier said than done.

Like King Solomon, I have trusted God through it all and God's hands have kept me through all of this time. I have been blessed with many lasting things. For example, I do not remember the names, faces, the racial background, or even the friends of the two girls that robbed me. I do not have any hate in my heart to cling to from this situation because it is not there. It is crazy and amazing that God wiped out that specific part of the memory. Second, I tend to make attempts to help people support themselves (even if it is someone I genuinely do not like). The last thing shows the most amazing power of God: since I thought books were so important in my life, I write them now.

Be encouraged and remain strong. You have made mistakes and I have too. However, God is a loving, forgiving God. He has forgotten your sins once you confessed them and asked for forgiveness. They are as far from your track record as hell is away from heaven. Please do not hold on to something that God himself had forgiven and forgotten. Share God's grace by forgiving someone that may have robbed you. Ask forgiveness from the ones from whom you've stolen.

REFERENCES

All scripture quotations are taken from the *New King James Bible* which was originally published by Thomas Nelson in 1975:

[1] John 17:1-26

[2] John 18:6

[3] Luke 23:34

[4] Luke 23:39

[5] Luke 23:40-42

[6] Luke 23:43

[7] John 19:28

[8] John 19:30

[9] Luke 23:47

[10] Matthew 27:51-53

[11] 1 Corinthians 3:11-15

ABOUT THE AUTHOR

In January 2013, I received the idea to write from God. I was shocked. It was something that I wanted to do, yet I found trouble finding the time to write this book. I had finished college with a degree in finance and accounting and landed a job working for a great publicly traded financial services firm. I was content with my life, or so it seemed. My wife and I were newlyweds and earned a good living. It seemed that we started out on the right foot in our marriage since we did 'all of the right things.' So I wondered: why did God want me to paint a picture of a life completely different than this?

As I continued working my demanding job, I found myself struggling with writers block in addition to my lack of writing time. I became frustrated with my slow progress on the book. Then, in November 2013, the unthinkable happened: I was unexpectedly laid off from my job. Immediately I began to ask myself: how long would it take for me to find another job? Would our savings be enough to cover our expenses? How was I going to afford the Hawaiian honeymoon I had planned?

At this time God raised the biggest question I ever faced in my life: would I choose to continue to live an honest life or would I choose to steal from someone? This question set the tone for how I conducted myself and I finished my first manuscript five months later. I wrote everyday starting on the day I was laid off, and I haven't skipped a day since that fateful day. Writing has officially become my mission, my purpose, my passion, and my therapy.

32376512R00094

Made in the USA
San Bernardino, CA
04 April 2016